BUILD

UNIVERSES

William A. Pollard

Behind Rose Bordered Windows

europe books

ISBN 9791220143387
First edition: September 2023

Behind Rose Bordered Windows

To Sophie, Adam, Kelley, Hayley, Ashar…
And Kimberley who likes to be called Kim.
My grandchildren… What a bunch of characters they are!
Everyone cherished by Sheila and myself for the joy they
bring to us. May their fortunes favour them for all time.

ACKNOWLEDGEMENTS

My thanks to my good friends Linda Heap, Marie Brewer, and John Cook. They all read the draft version of this book and they have all returned to me with lots of positive and constructive comments and suggestions.

At the risk of embarrassing Sheila, my wife of over 52 years, I would like to give her a special mention, with my appreciation for all the encouragement she has given me. She has read, re-read and read again every word of every chapter of all my books to help me to prepare them for publishing. Her patience when correcting my idiot mistakes never ceased to amaze me and her words of wisdom helped me make sense of my thoughts and ponderings while searching for words to write.

Thank you, all, for your help.

PROLOGUE

Summer, 1740.

Farmer Willum Colbert is forty years old. He inherited Colbert's farm from his father who, in turn, had the farm passed down to him by his father. In fact, the farm was initially started as a smallholding way back in the late 1500s, three generations earlier than Willum.

Willum is not rich in comparison to the landed gentry surrounding his farm, but neither is he short of a bob or two. Financial acumen and shrewd farm management over the years had enabled the Colbert's to expand the farm to its present size, about twenty-five square miles (sixteen thousand acres).

Willum and his wife, Lydia, and his two children are preparing for their summer vegetable harvest. Willum's farm is, predominantly, a livestock farm but also with many acres of arable fields to grow hay, wheat and vegetables. This produce sees his family and his livestock through the long dark winters until he can corral his sheep in time for the shearing season.

Consigning the original farmhouse to storage he built a palatial farm cottage to live in, a manor house by all accounts, together with five smaller cottages all situated in a corner of the estate in one of his less productive fields. Colbert's Field. A Trout stream bubbled its way past the cottages and meandered its way through the estate to some unseen part of the country.

From this manor he managed the farm. The little hamlet housed the farm hands that help to milk the cows, shear the sheep, harvest the hay and crops, and maintain the farm.

His wife and children fed the pigs and hens and goats and all the other farm animals that eventually get taken to the town market when they are fat enough to be sold.

Willum's father had generously donated a large sum of money to the village, a short distance from the farm, to enable its longevity and future expansion. The villages had re-named the village 'Colbert' in recognition of his generosity.

Willum and his family live a happy, comfortable life and he ensures that his workforce is happy because he feeds them, pays them a handsome bonus each year and provides the cottages which shelter them from the harsh winters. They all worked hard to make Willum's farm productive.

Unfortunately, despite his hard work Willum's farm falls on bad times. In the space of four years, he lost everything… Everything except his son.

In 1745 there was a drought. Rain clouds didn't darken the skies at all that year or the next. His crops shrivelled back into the parched earth and several of his sheep died of dehydration. His cows stopped giving milk and had to be put down.

Throughout 1747 torrential rain drowned every one of his meagre crops and flooded the farm to the extent that almost half his remaining herd of sheep drowned. Many more died through starvation. There was little left to take to market.

By the end of that year his farm hands had all deserted Willum because he could not feed them or pay their wages. They left their picturesque cottages empty and lifeless.

By the middle of 1749 Willum was broken. His daughter had died of pneumonia during the floods and his wife had died of old age earlier in the year. Growing old, and with just a teenage son, he was unable to properly manage the farm and bring it back to its former glory, so the farm became neglected and run down.

As a consequence of what had happened in those previous four years Willum became saddled with debt. He could no longer buy feed for his livestock and so he had to sell what livestock he had left after the floods. With no income he could no longer afford to run his farm and he found it necessary to gradually sell packets of this to the landed gentry. They had all watched Willum's demise over the years but offered no help. In fact, they had constantly rubbed their greedy, sweaty palms together in the knowledge that if they waited long enough, they could pick up sixteen thousand acres of prime land for a pittance.

Willum saw his life's work gradually fragmented before his eyes until there was just one field left. Colbert's Field, with a manor house and five cottages and a bubbling Trout stream.

When Willum died in 1751 his fifteen-year-old son, Willum junior, was taken to the poor house. Back in the day few records of ownership were kept so there were few records of Willum junior's inheritance. Willum junior didn't have anyone to fight for his rights, and he was too young to fight for them himself. He never knew that Willum senior had willed him Colbert's Field, together with a manor house, five cottages, a bubbling Trout stream and a handsome pot of two hundred pounds. This inheritance represented the residue of property and cash from the sale of the farm after paying off Willum's debts.

The original will, made when Willum junior was born, was held in trust by a London solicitor who was never told that Willum had died or that his heir had been sent to the poor house. As soon as the will was ratified it was consigned to the solicitor's dusty archives and Willum, his son and Colbert's Field were all but forgotten.

Colbert's Field with its manor house and five cottages and a bubbling Trout stream lay dormant, silent and unwanted for several centuries.

PART 1

ENLIGHTENMENT

Chapter 1

William Franklin Colbert, Bill to those who knew him, was born in 1978. He is from a long line of Williams, whose name had been passed down for generations.

He is a private investigator. Not an investigator in terms of divorce or murder, but an investigator of stolen jewellery. His work involves tracking down and returning stolen high value jewellery for the insurance companies. He was occasionally sent abroad to locate and recover the expensive possessions… Diamond bracelets, tiaras, real pearl necklaces, emerald brooches and the like. You know? The stuff that few people can afford and is kept locked inside a dark safe at home, supposedly well-hidden and burglar proof.

He is good at his job. He's a successful and popular businessman with an office in Surrey, a Partner and several employees and he owns a super expensive car. At forty-four years old he had done well, his comfortable lifestyle existing not least due to his hard work but also due to the support from his first and only love, Amelia. She preferred to be called Amy.

He was twenty-one years old and single when they met in 1999. A dance hall in Richmond had brought them together while Bill was on a bender with some of his mates, celebrating a stag night in London. Bill's tanned film-star looks, blonde wavy hair and sculptured physique captured Amy's attention the moment he entered the room. She was there with some of her friends on a 'girls-night-out'. For her it was love at first sight as the room and everyone in it disappeared in a haze as she sat at her table, staring in awe at Bill's self-assured magnetism.

The other women at Amy's table gasped in wonderment as they whispered amongst themselves.

"Look at that dreamboat," said one.

"He's an Angel," volunteered another.

"No. He's a God," whispered her friend.

"Somebody wake me up," someone else muttered.

Her friend said, dreamily, "Who'd go to sleep with him in bed next to them?" encouraging lots of 'Ooooh's, from the girls.

"Too rich for you lot," joked another, inducing chuckles of laughter around the table.

Amy didn't hear any of this banter as she gazed wide eyed at Bill surveying the room with his mates, looking round for a vacant table.

"There's one," his pal said, pointing to an empty table with enthusiasm. The vacant table was next to Amy's table and every one of the girl's party looked at each other in surprised anticipation. Maybe this girls-night-out would prove to be better than they first imagined.

As the night progressed so did the men. After a few dances, several drinks and some awkward introductions they pushed the two tables together and melded the two parties into one, all eager to have a good time dancing and perhaps have a better time when the dancing had finished. Bill and Amy talked and stared into each other's eyes throughout the evening.

"Ahhhh… They're in love," laughed their friends.

"Yeah, she's taken a big fall," someone in the crowd joked.

From the moment Bill first saw Amy he knew he was going to marry her. His first thoughts of the lovely vision before him were 'She's gorgeous,' thoughts that he repeated every time he looked at her in all the years, they were together.

From that night onwards, Bill and Amy spent as much time together as their jobs permitted, despite Bill's intermittent trips abroad. They were hopelessly in love and became inseparable. Marriage was definitely on the cards and in May 2002, two years after Bill's own stag night, their daughter, Elizabeth May Colbert, was born.

When Elizabeth reached her teenage years, she insisted that everyone called her Elle, perhaps a teenage fad that she had picked up from school. The nickname stuck with her as she grew up to become as beautiful and as self-assured as Amy. Now twenty years old, Elle has sailed through her education, excelled at university and is now employed as a highly influential marketing executive in Bill's firm. The clients love her, her workmates love her, and Bill loves her.

Amy and Elle are mirror images of each other and frequently meet up for lunch. They always giggle childishly when strangers mistake them for sisters and the young men hit on Amy as if she was still footloose and fancy-free.

In fact, Amy flirted with the young men more than Elle, but they both knew that flirting was just a bit of harmless fun.

With Elle now living in a flat with her best friend life could not be better for Bill and Amy as they snuggled down in the home, they had made for themselves in Kensington, London.

March 2022.

As lunch time approached Bill dashed out of his office, down the corridor, through the fire door and down the fire escape stairway. Bouncing down the stairs three at a time while holding onto the handrail he emerged, just a few seconds later, into the bright sunlight bathing the street with its warmth. He was late for a lunch date with Amy, so he crashed along the crowded pavement, barging people out of the way and shouting a repetitive "Sorry," over his shoulder to each one of those that he had pushed aside.

Amelia sat at the table in the restaurant softly drumming her fingers on the tablecloth and looking intently out of the window. She had earlier asked Bill to join her for lunch because she had something 'important' to tell him and she was now beginning to get a little impatient with Bill's late arrival. She had expected him to meet her outside the restaurant but decided, instead, to sit inside at their pre-booked table.

Bill entered the restaurant in a less dignified way, crashing back the door and knocking a pedestal of flowers over. An embarrassing silence descended on the diners who all looked in Bill's direction to see what the commotion was about. Apologising to everyone he squeezed passed as he made his way to Amy's table he stood in front of her, waiting for the reprimand for being late that he surely deserved.

"Sorry," he offered to her, but he could see that that wasn't enough atonement for his lateness as he bent down to give her a kiss.

Bending down, his arse pushed over a bottle of red wine which in turn knocked over a full wine glass, spilling the contents of the bottle and glass over the adjacent tablecloth. The occupants of that table hurriedly stood up to dodge the spilled wine and muttered profanities at Bill. He

turned to see what that commotion was about and sheep-
ishly apologised for his clumsiness.

"Sorry…"

That didn't cut it with his neighbours whose stare
would have melted a block of ice had one been in front of
them.

Amy's face was a picture of exasperation and in a matter of
fact tone told Bill to, "Sit down and stop making a fuss."

Chapter 2

In the soft lighting of the restaurant Bill and Amy talked intimately as they sat waiting for their pre-lunch drinks. They both had some news to announce.

Eager to find out what was so important, Bill got straight to the point and asked, "So, what's the news?"

"No, you first," smiled Amy.

"Ah, I've received a letter from some solicitor's office in London. He wants me to pay him a visit to discuss something about a field."

"What about the field?"

"Don't know. He didn't go into details, but he did say that a meeting would be to my benefit if I could spare half-an-hour."

Amy thought for a moment, absorbing what Bill had just said.

"Could be something about buried jewellery that he wants you to dig up," she joked.

"Nah," Bill replied. "If it was that I'm sure he wouldn't have been so cagey about discussing it."

Bill shrugged his shoulders in submission. "Doesn't matter."

The drinks and the menu arrived and after a few minutes of menu gazing they gave their meal order to the waitress. She hurried away to pass the order on to the chef.

"Okay, what is this news that you've been itching to tell me since this morning?" questioned Bill.

Amy paused for a moment while she thought how she could put the news to Bill.

Buttering her bread bun, she suddenly blurted out, "I've been promoted," as if the words had been stuck in her mouth and they had just decided to free themselves.

"Wow. What's your new title? Assistant mail room letter sorter?" Bill joked.

Amy threw a piece of her bread bun at him in mock anger.

"David's promoted me to science Editor," she proudly smiled. "I'll have a team of 3 gofers to assist me and make the tea."

"Phew!" Bill teased. "I have to make my own tea."

With excited chat Amy described what her new job entailed while they both enjoyed their lunch and, indeed, each other's company. Lunch dates were few and far between nowadays.

Since her marriage to Bill, Amy had been working part time at home while bringing up Elle.

She had been employed as a proof-reader by Globe Publications, a publishing house located in London. She didn't do the job for the money. Bill's income easily kept her and Elle in the lifestyle that they all enjoyed, but she needed something to keep her mind active while being the devoted mother that she was. Something that didn't necessitate daily office incarceration while she brought up Elle.

With a degree in English languages, she was snapped up by the publishing house immediately she applied for the job, and she had enjoyed proof-reading the huge variety of manuscripts that had been sent to her by David March, the firm's MD.

As soon as Elle 'flew the nest' to go to university, Amy had persuaded David to give her a permanent job in the office. She continued as proof-reader to the science department and became well respected by her co-workers.

Fifty-five-year-old Hugo was the fiction department proof-reader. A working friendship with Amy developed as they sat in the canteen during their lunch breaks, discussing the manuscripts that they had been tasked with amending.

One morning the science Editor suffered a major stroke and keeled over during a meeting with David. Such was the severity of his stroke, the Editor never regained consciousness and sadly passed away in hospital a few hours later.

Amy was initially asked to stand in as acting Editor while a replacement could be found. She mentioned this role to Bill during an evening meal at home, but little credence was placed on its significance.

Amy settled into her new temporary role with ease.

Having spent several years as a proof-reader it was, to her, a natural progression to make. But progression always comes hand-in-hand with sacrifice.

In a position of responsibility, one has to accept that it's not always possible to put loved ones first. She had accepted this fact when she married Bill because she knew that he would be away from home, sometimes for two or three days, while he chased down an expensive bit of bling somewhere in Europe. Now it was her turn to tell Bill that she would not be there to cuddle up to him in bed.

She often had to travel to far off cities to meet up with a book agent, or to research a location described by an author in his manuscript and over time both Bill and Amy started to become accustomed to lonely nights and solo breakfasts. It was part of their jobs and they both acknowledged that being apart for some of the time was necessary.

David accompanied her on most of her field trips.

During this period David watched her closely. Would she be able to handle the responsibility of leadership?

Would her subordinates accept her as their leader? Would she make the right decisions?

After several months of being a stand in Editor she was called to David's office to be given the good news. With Amy's reputation of being a diligent, well liked and respected worker David had no hesitation in persuading the Board that she should be the one promoted to lead the science department.

The news came as bit of a shock, not just to Amy but to the whole office as everyone had always eyed Hugo up as the next Editor-in-waiting. When David announced the promotion Hugo was laid-back by it and warmly joined the line of workers queueing to congratulate Amy.

Bill treated Amy and Elle to a night out at the theatre to celebrate Amy's promotion. They all then went to Bill's favourite restaurant for a slap-up meal. To top-up the celebration Bill took the women to a disco where, much to Bill's amusement, Amy and Elle flirted with the young men whilst gyrating and bouncing up and down on the dance floor in apparent abandonment. Bill propped up the bar. The night was one of joy and laughter. A night to remember. When they eventually left the disco hall in the early hours of the morning they prowled the streets, searching for a taxi to take them home.

As the taxi turned into the street where Bill lived, he caught sight of a man running down the four entry steps to his front door. Dressed in a dark hoody, Bill didn't see the man's face as he turned away from the approaching taxi and raced down the street. Not wishing to spoil the evening for the girls, Bill kept quiet to let them continue their light banter and semi-drunk laughter.

After pulling up at the kerb in front of the house Bill paid the taxi driver, swung his legs out of the car and pulled himself upright on the pavement. Standing there, watching the man run round the distant street corner and disappear from sight, he wondered what the man had been doing at his front door. Leaving the girls to get themselves out of the car he walked up the steps and inspected the door. It was still tightly closed and locked.

Hearing jibes of "Always the polite person…," he turned to assist his giggling family up the steps and into the house.

It took Bill several hours to shake a feeling of unease as a vision of the intruder running down his entry steps kept appearing inside his head. He slept intermittently until it was time to shower and dress for work the following morning.

After a routine day at work, he returned home to scrutinise the video playback from the previous night. The event had unnerved him all day and he wanted to see if the intruder could be recognised. No chance. The intruder's hoody covered his face. What Bill did see, however, was the person about to put what appeared to be a key into the door lock when he suddenly turned, peered down the street and fled down the steps.

Did he have a key to the door? Why did he have a key to the door? Where did he get the key?

Bill downloaded the video onto a memory stick and then deleted it from the recorder. He decided to take the memory stick to his mate in the Met Police to see what advice his mate could give.

"Everything all right?" Amy asked as she wandered past Bill, head down in the cupboard furtively pressing buttons on the video recorder.

"Yep. Just checking things," answered Bill lightly so as not to worry Amy.

He put the memory stick into his pocket and phoned his secretary to let her know that he will not be in the office tomorrow.

He then phoned his mate in the Met to arrange a meeting.

Chapter 3

The following morning Inspector Walter (Wally) Coombes ushered Bill into his office and asked his secretary for coffee. Bill sat across Wally's cluttered desk and they both chatted about nothing in particular until the tray, with a pot of steaming coffee and a plate of biscuits arrived and was placed between them.

"What's the problem?" asked Wally.

Bill took out the memory stick and passed it across the desk to Wally.

"Take a look," prompted Bill, and Wally plugged the memory stick into the USB port on his laptop.

Giving Wally a couple of minutes to view the video Bill asked, "What do you reckon?"

After a pause, while Wally reflected on the video, he removed the memory stick and turned to Bill.

"He's an interesting character, isn't he? Can I hang on to this?" he asked. "I'll see if one of our techies can clean up the image. We may be able to get a clearer picture of his face."

"No problem. What are the chances of a collar?" questioned Bill.

"Not a lot," answered Wally. "Hoodies like that are as common as farts in a toilet, but we might be lucky. I'll let you know."

Leaving Wally's office, he summoned a taxi and went to the solicitor's office.

Symonds, Baker & Stace, LLP, are located in an olde-worlde quadrant just off The Strand, London. The firm proudly displays a banner on their letter-head pronouncing 'Established in 1735'. Starting off as a one-man band in a picturesque village in East Anglia called Colbert the legal firm had, over the centuries, been passed down to offspring, been bought, been passed down some more, bought some more and was now absorbed into an expensive solicitor's practice in this quaint, archaic corner of London.

Bill entered the office and was immediately confronted by a receptionist's desk, behind which sat a young lady in a smart two-piece suit smiling at him.

"My name's Bill Colbert. I have an appointment with Nigel Stace."

Glancing at her PC Screen and tapping a few keys she looked up at Bill and said, "Good afternoon, Mr. Colbert. Please take a seat while I let Mr. Stace know you've arrived. Would you like a cup of tea or coffee?"

"Coffee would be great, thanks," Bill replied and made himself comfortable in one of the art deco chairs beckoning him.

The receptionist picked up her telephone and pressed a speed-dial button.

"Your next appointment has arrived," she stated after a short pause, then she disclosed who was sat waiting in front of her. "Mr. Colbert."

Replacing the telephone handset, she stood up and made her way to the coffee pot standing on a corner table, at the same time letting Bill know, "Mr. Stace will be with you shortly."

Nigel Stace was every inch the Victorian solicitor that Bill had imagined when he first walked into the olde-worlde quadrant.

He was a small, balding man with a stoop. Rimless spectacles were perched on the end of his nose and with shirt sleeve holders above his elbows, waistcoat, spats covering the tops of Victorian style shoes it seemed that he had just been launched through a wormhole from the 1800s. Warmly greeting Bill, he ushered him into the solicitor's den.

Taking a seat in the plush buttoned Victorian chair, Bill waited patiently while Nigel rummaged through the tower of files adorning the corner of his desk until he found the one, he was looking for. Sitting opposite Bill he opened the file and smiled a gleaming white smile.

"Thank you for coming here, this afternoon, Mr. Colbert."

"It's my pleasure. Please, call me Bill."

"Well, Bill, it seems that you have inherited some land close to your namesake village of Colbert."

"Didn't know there was such a place. Where is it?"

"The village is in East Anglia," informed Nigel. "I have the location here for you," passing Bill a slip of paper with all the relevant details neatly typed on it.

"Apparently," continued Nigel, "the land in question consists of a single field with the name of 'Colbert's Field', located on the outskirts of the village. The field has been dormant for centuries and it was only by good fortune that we came across this inheritance in our archives."

"Oh? Tell me more," chuckled Bill.

Nigel produced an ancestry chart and gave Bill a potted history of the time Willum Colbert willed the land to his son. How that will had been archived and how those archives had lounged, forgotten, in a dusty barn on the outskirts of London until the solicitor's practice was bought out by a London-based firm. The archives had, once more, laid dormant and forgotten as it was passed around the various practice owners until its absorption by Symonds, Baker & Stace in 2018. It had taken two years to audit all the archives and a further two years to research the history of

Colbert's field to ascertain its present ownership. Bill Colbert is now the last remaining successor to Willum Colbert's legacy of Colbert's Field.

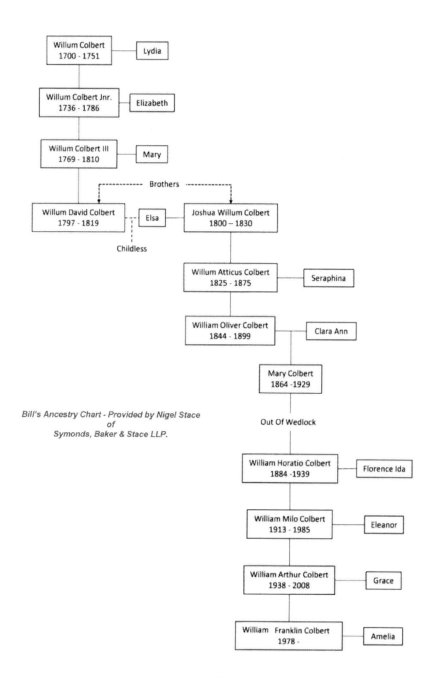

| Willum Colbert 1700 - 1751 | — | Lydia |

| Willum Colbert Jnr. 1736 - 1786 | — | Elizabeth |

| Willum Colbert III 1769 - 1810 | — | Mary |

---------- Brothers ----------

| Willum David Colbert 1797 - 1819 | — | Elsa | — | Joshua Willum Colbert 1800 – 1830 |

Childless

| Willum Atticus Colbert 1825 - 1875 | — | Seraphina |

| William Oliver Colbert 1844 - 1899 | — | Clara Ann |

| Mary Colbert 1864 -1929 |

Bill's Ancestry Chart - Provided by Nigel Stace
of
Symonds, Baker & Stace LLP.

Out Of Wedlock

| William Horatio Colbert 1884 -1939 | — | Florence Ida |

| William Milo Colbert 1913 - 1985 | — | Eleanor |

| William Arthur Colbert 1938 - 2008 | — | Grace |

| William   Franklin Colbert 1978 - | — | Amelia |

Bill sat back in his chair, gently cradled his chin and rubbed his cheek with his index finger while he considered Nigel's words. After a few silent moments he spoke up.

"A field... This poses a few questions. How large is the field? Is there anything on it by way of buildings or crops? What about access? Are there any preserved access rights by anyone?"

Nigel looked over his spectacles and answered the questions as best he could.

"Our researcher has been able to ascertain that the field is approximately six hectares in size. That's about fifteen acres. It's not a massive field, but it may have some potential for building on. We haven't uncovered any liens, loans or building applications, and we haven't found any rights of ownership except yours, so it is safe to say that the field is yours to do with as you wish. Other than that, we have no more information to give you."

After a pause Nigel continued, "You will, of course, need to obtain building regulations approval if you want to build on it or you could just sell the land to a property developer."

"A field...," Bill repeated, more to himself than to the solicitor. "Is that it?" he asked.

Nigel smiled his best smile and answered, "Actually, there is more."

Bill sat back with raised eyebrows in anticipation of the information Nigel was about to pass on to him.

"The Farmer, Willum Colbert, bequeathed a sum of two hundred pounds to his son that has been held in trust since, and has never been claimed. In today's terms it amounts to about fifty-five thousand pounds."

Bill let out a long breath and thought about the afternoon's discussion.

After a few moments he looked at Nigel and asked, "Where do I sign?"

Bill spent about half-an-hour in the local library researching Colbert's Field.

There were numerous books on the history of Colbert village and a couple on Colbert's Farm. The only document on Colbert's field, however, was a map of the area dated 1630, prior to Willum's ownership, indicating where the field was in relation to the village and original farmhouse.

He returned home to give the news to Amy.

Walking up the steps leading to his front door Bill saw something out of the corner of his eye that made him quickly turn his head. Turning the distant street corner, he was sure that he a saw hoody disappear from view.

Bill stood there for a moment trying to picture what he thought he had just seen. He could be wrong…But he was pretty damned sure that it was the same hoody that had tried to enter his home the previous day.

He decided not to upset Amy with his suspicions and entered his home in a jovial, upbeat mode.

Amy listened with interest to the playback of Bill's day.

"Are you going to look at it?" she asked, referring to the field.

"Not yet," answered Bill, "I'll wait for the legal stuff to be completed."

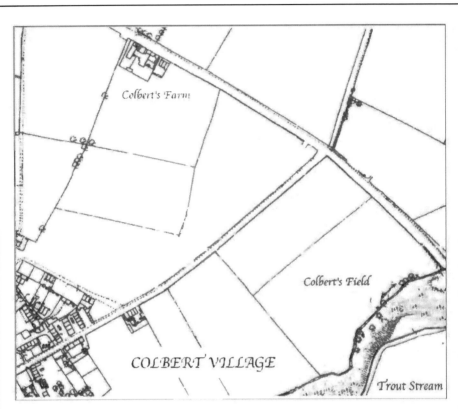

Map of Colbert Village before Willum inherited the farm, dated 1630, showing the original farmhouse and Colbert's Field where Willum built his manor house and five cottages.

Chapter 4

August 2022.

It took three months for Symonds, Baker & Stace, LLP, to finalise the legalities for ownership of Colbert's Field. Bill and Amy were on a much-deserved summer holiday when the documentation was pushed through their letterbox in late July.

After a tiring, red-eye flight back to the UK and a lengthy taxi ride the two arrived home and lugged their suitcases up the entry steps.

Bill inserted his key into the front door lock, turned it and pushed the door open. A pile of correspondence sat on the doormat, awaiting their return.

Bending down to gather up the mail Bill noticed a well-defined footprint, stretching across several of the envelopes. Someone had clearly stood on the pile of envelopes shortly after it had rained and left a muddy footmark. Somebody with a key to the door.

Before she left for the airport Amy had asked Elle to call in occasionally to check the house over while they were away. Assuming Elle had carelessly trampled on the mail Bill muttered to Amy, "You'd think that she could have picked this lot up for us, wouldn't you?"

The mail was sorted into Bill's mail and Amy's mail on the dining table. Leaving his for a more convenient time, Bill heaved the suitcases upstairs and put them in the bedroom to be unpacked after they had had some lunch. Amy phoned Elle to invite her over for a chat and a photo display about the holiday, then went upstairs to unpack. Bill prioritised his mail, chucking the junk mail into the recycling bin, and returned upstairs to help Amy unpack.

A little later the doorbell announced the arrival of Elle. She welcomed Amy home with a hug and then gave Bill a peck on his cheek. Bill then took his mail into the kitchen to open and read while the girls chatted about the holiday. Out of earshot, he read the unimportant stuff and put this into a pile for onwards transmission to Amy.

He held the solicitor's heavy envelope in his hand cogitating over its contents. It felt as if there was something bulky inside. Tearing off the top of the envelope he poured the contents onto the kitchen worktop. It dropped with a clang and bounced. It was a rusty old door key. A large key, similar to the ones seen in antique shops... Too big to keep in one's pocket and with a decorative Bow and Blade, clearly a very old door key. Bill dropped the key back into the envelope and made a mental note to fully read and digest the contents of the paperwork that accompanied it as soon as time permitted.

He didn't hear Elle apologies to Amy that she had been unable to visit the house during their absence.

The three of them had a jovial restaurant lunch, Amy constantly imparting funny anecdotes to Elle about their stay in Bermuda.

After lunch Bill summoned a taxi to take the girls home and then made his way to the office to pick up any messages that might need an immediate answer.

Entering the office he bent down to Julie, his secretary, and whispered into her ear, "I'm on holiday until tomorrow."

She nodded in acknowledgement with a smile.

With little by way of important messages Bill went round to see his Partner.

"Hi, Bill. Have a good time?" enquired his partner, Brad Somerton.

"Fantastic," replied Bill, "any problems?"

"Nope, not one. A Belgium insurer has sent us an interesting job. Recovery of a book of rare stamps nicked from a footballer's home in Eindhoven, where-ever that is. Do you want it? I'll take it if you're not interested but it'll have to wait until next week. I'm a bit bogged down with that report on the Rolex we recovered a couple of weeks ago."

"How much we talking about?" asked Bill.

"They didn't want to talk much over the phone, but they did mention it was a six-figure sum."

"Yeah, okay. Ask Julie to arrange a meeting with them and flights for me. I'll have a look at the paperwork tomorrow."

"No probs. How did you get on with your solicitor guy? Are you a man of substantial means, yet?" joked Brad.

"Yes, apparently. I now own a field somewhere in Essex. The paperwork arrived at my place while we were on holiday, but I've not yet had chance to read it."

Brad joked, "Take up camping…"

Bill had known Brad since their university days.

They had both taken an instant liking for each other and their friendship had spilled over into their respective family lives. They frequently visited each other's homes to chat, have BBQ's, gossip and have fun and they both had keys to the other's door, for emergencies, although neither of them had ever had any reason to use their key. They had set up their company, Colbert & Somerton, shortly after leaving university.

With the footprint on his mail in mind, Bill asked Brad if he had been to his place while he and Amy had been away.

"Nope," answered Brad, "Why do you ask?"

Bill told Brad about his encounters with hoody, and the footprint on his mail.

"Who else has got a key to your door?" enquired Brad.

"Only Elle and the cleaner," confirmed Bill. "But the cleaner is in her seventies so she wouldn't be able to dash from the house like hoody. Amy did ask Elle to visit while we were away, though."

"Well, there you have it. It is obviously Elle's footprint, but I don't know what I can tell you about hoody. Have you been to see Wally?"

Inspector Wally Coombes was another of their close friends from Uni.

"Yes, but he doesn't hold out much hope of catching the bugger without a positive I.D."

"Not much you can do, old boy, except wait until Wally comes up with something. Take your mind off it and go visit your vast estate in Essex."

"Yeah…Probably a good idea."

After some more chit-chat and coffee Bill left the office to go home.

On his way-out Julie gave him details of his meeting, the day after tomorrow in Belgium.

Chapter 5

Bill sat in the waiting room of the Belgium insurer's office.

His mobile phone vibrated in his pocket, indicating an inbound text to him. It was Elle.

'Where are you,' she texted.

The secretary's phone rang, and she picked up the receiver.

'In Belgium,' Bill replied to Elle.

Just as he was about to read Elle's next text the secretary advised him that, "Mr. Dupont is ready for you now, Mr. Colbert."

Bill turned his phone to silent ring, put it back in his pocket and followed the secretary into Mr. Dupont's plush office.

The meeting went well. Dupont had already collated sufficient information to start an investigation and he handed the file over to Bill. The two men clearly took a liking to each other, and they sat and chatted while coffee was brought in and poured into China cups. Terms of engagement and a fee was agreed, and they both sat back, satisfied with the day's meeting. They chatted about work, their families, the weather… Mundane things while they enjoyed their coffee and relaxed.

As they passed the time of day, Bill's phone kept vibrating to notify him of incoming texts. After several missed text messages, he decided to find out who was so anxious to talk to him. Retrieving his phone, he apologised to Dupont.

"I'm terribly sorry, but someone is pestering me to talk. Do you mind if I get this?"

"No, not at all. Please, go ahead," Dupont smiled as he considerately left the room to give Bill some privacy.

Bill looked down at the missed calls. They were all from Elle.

"Dad, can you call back asap?"

"Dad, I need you to call back."

"Dad please call back. We need to talk."

"Please, dad, please call me. This is important."

There was also a text from Brad.

"Bill, phone Elle urgently."

With a furrowed brow Bill pressed the speed dial key and waited for Elle to respond.

"Dad! Thank goodness. I've been trying to call you for ages."

"Yes, I know. Sorry about that. I was in the middle of a meeting."

"You have to come home," Elle urged. "Mom's had an accident."

Bill fired off several questions in quick succession.

"What? What kind of accident? Is she all right? How bad is it? …"

"I'm with her at the hospital," Elle interjected.

"What happened?" pressed Bill.

"Got to go. I'll explain all later," Elle announced.

"Wait! What's happening?" questioned Bill.

"I'll call later," hurried Elle, then Bill's phone went dead.

He couldn't do any more until Elle called back so Bill exited the office, thanked Dupont for his hospitality and confirmed that he would instigate his investigation straight away.

"Are you okay?" Dupont queried. "You don't look too good," he volunteered. "How was your telephone call?"

"Oh, it's nothing," answered Bill. "Just a minor domestic crisis. I'm sure I'll be able to deal with it when I get home."

"That's good. I'll let you get along, then. Give my regards to Amy when you get home and keep me in the loop about our missing book of stamps."

"Of course." Bill smiled.

Bill left the office with an uneasy feeling that he was sure he heard Elle crying. Maybe not, but he decided to wait for her return call before asking.

He had originally banked on making his initial enquiries in Belgium, where the theft took place, but on reflection he decided to cut his visit short and get an earlier flight back to the U.K. It would mean a duplicated visit, with extra costs, but in view of Elle's insistence to return home he thought that was a more important request to fulfil.

While waiting to board his plane for the return trip home he telephoned Brad. Perhaps he could shed some light on Elle's frantic call.

"Hi, Bill. Where are you?"

"I'm at the airport waiting to board my flight home. Tell Julie she did a good job."

"Will do. How'd the meeting go?"

"Went well. I've got all the instructions we need to begin the investigation."

"Good. I'll instruct Dominic to make a start. Dupont's already emailed the executive summary."

Bill was puzzled by Brad's response. He appeared to have made a unilateral decision to take this job from him and hand it to his assistant.

"What do you know about Elle's call to me?" questioned Bill.

Brad detected a hint of animosity in Bill's question.

"Elle? Oh, not a lot. She apparently got a call from someone, dashed into my office and just said that she had to go out. She asked me to tell you to call her, in case you called me first."

Brad continued, *'Dad's going to be out of the office for a while,'* was all she said. If you're going to be out of the office for a while, I thought it best to start the investigation as soon as possible. That's why I got Dominic on the case. Is that okay with you?"

"Oh. Yeah," Bill replied, absentmindedly. "So, you don't know anything about Amy's accident?"

"No. God, no! What accident? Elle never said. I've no idea how serious it is. Do you know? Do you want me to do anything?"

"Don't know myself, but don't trouble Elle with phone calls yet. I'll find out when I get back. I've got to go, Brad. Elle's trying to phone me."

"Okay. Talk to you when you get in."

Bill terminated that call and immediately answered Elle.

"Hi, Elle. What's the score?"

"I'll tell you when you get home. I've got your flight details and I'll pick you up at the airport."

With that Elle cut the call connection and immediately turned her phone off. Bill was now convinced that Elle was crying when she made that last call. Why? Why had she cut the call off before Bill could answer?

On the surface it appeared that something serious had happened, and Bill had a frustrating wait until his flight landed and Elle met him at the arrivals lounge.

Greeting each other with a hug, Bill could see that Elle had been distressed and crying.

"What's wrong?" he asked.

Elle looked at Bill for a long time. She broke into staccato sobs as tears ran down her face. Bill ushered her over to a bench, sat them both down and waited while she regained a little composure.

With a tearful sob she blurted out, "Mum's dead."

Bill held his daughter close to him and listened to her uncontrolled sobs as he tried to comprehend what she had just told him.

When Elle eventually regained full control of her emotions she sat back, blew her nose and looked at Bill for response to her statement.

Bill asked, "What happened?"

"There was a fire at home. It was so bad that mum couldn't get out. The ambulance man told me that she may not have suffered too much because she was probably unconscious due to smoke inhalation before the flames reached her."

"Where did they take her?"

"She was air lifted to University College Hospital."

"How did you find out?"

"Our neighbour phoned me. I dashed to your place to find the road blocked off by the police. Wally was there and he allowed me in to be with her until the helicopter arrived."

Elle paused for a breath. "Dad, she was in a terrible state. She had been burnt all over," Sobbed Elle. "I couldn't even identify her. She was this black, charred… Thing… She had no face…Just burnt flesh… Everywhere."

Elle sat forward and vomited on the floor in front of her, her coughing interrupted by sobs. When she had, once more, composed herself Bill went to fetch a cup of water from a nearby water dispenser.

Handing the cup to Elle he said, "let's go home. I'll decide what to do next when we get there."

"You can't," Elle shouted. "There is no more home... It doesn't exist... It's been burnt to the ground," she cried.

Chapter 6

Bill took Elle back to her flat. They were met by Janice, Elle's flat mate.

Elle offered Bill the couch for the night as he now had nowhere to live. The offer was gratefully accepted, and Bill went out to find an all-night garage to buy some essentials. He didn't go straight back to the flat. Instead, he decided to go home to see what state it was in. The police cordon was still in place but after showing some I.D. Bill was allowed access.

Elle had been right. The house was now, indeed, a pile of rubble. Bill phoned Brad to bring him up to speed, at the same time asking if the company car could be delivered to Elle's flat in the morning.

"No problem, old boy," confirmed Brad, "Is there anything else I can do?"

"Can you arrange for the office flat to be made available? I'm staying at Elle's place tonight, but I'll need somewhere more permanent to stay."

The office had an accompanying flat within its rented space which was used by the employees if they worked late. The flat was self-managed, everyone taking their sheets, pillowcases and toiletries home with them when they had finished with the flat.

"I'll phone the housekeeper now to ask if she can get it ready for you," confirmed Brad. "No need to come in tomorrow. I've got things here under control."

"Thanks Brad. I'll need a bit of down time to get things sorted."

"No probs. Just turn up when you can."

"Will do."

With that Bill turned his phone off and made his way back to Elle's place for what turned out to be a disturbed night's sleep.

The following morning Bill phoned Wally to arrange a meeting. At ten a.m. sharp Bill was shown into Wally's office.

Wally started the conversation, "Morning, Bill. Where'd you sleep last night?"

"At Elle's. I've arranged to stay at the company flat from today so that I don't have to put up with your choice of TV programmes," joked Bill.

"Not mine... Ann keeps the TV control away from me." Ann is Wally's long-suffering wife.

Bill probed Wally for some answers. "Elle says she met you there last night. What can you tell me?"

"Not a lot, Bill. Elle phoned me at about seven p.m. to ask for my help. I sent a team down there to manage the place but by the time they arrived the fire and ambulance services were already on site. I followed on at about seven-thirty. That's when I met Elle."

"Have the Fire Brigade said what caused it?"

"Investigations are still on-going but, all things being considered, it's beginning to look like a gas explosion."

"Didn't anyone smell anything beforehand?"

"No reports of any gas leaks, but my lads conducted a house-to-house last night and the neighbours didn't have any indications of a leak."

"So, nobody saw, or heard anything until the explosion?"

"Correct..."

Wally paused and then opened the file in front of him with a furrowed brow.

"Actually, one of the homeowners in the adjacent street reported someone running towards the underground station," volunteered Wally while reading from the file.

"They heard the explosion at around six forty-five and poked their heads through the curtains to see your place in flames. They looked in the opposite direction and that's when they saw this chap running down the road. One of my men managed to get a copy of the homeowner's CCTV from about five p.m."

Wally picked up his telephone handset, dialled a number and spoke to his colleague.

"Jim, can you bring that CCTV download in here for me to look at?"

Replacing the handset, he confirmed that the CCTV film will arrive in a moment.

Wally continued, "Might be something, might be nothing."

"Yeah. When will you be closing your file on this?"

"Got to wait for the Fire Brigade's report and the post-mortem. If there's nothing in those reports, we'll have to mark it down as an accident."

"Okay. Keep me in the loop?"

"Of course."

A tap on Wally's door signalled the arrival of the CCTV video.

"Do you want to see this?" asked Wally.

"Sure. Why not?"

The memory stick was inserted into Wally's laptop, and he tapped a few keys to display the film on a large TV screen hanging from the wall opposite his desk.

Scrolling through the playback Bill and Wally noted the time of the explosion at six forty-five when the camera shook from the blast, just as the homeowner had said. Fifteen seconds later the runner was picked up by the camera running away from the homeowner's property towards the underground station, just as the homeowner had said.

Wally paused the film at that point. He and Bill looked at each other with raised eyebrows until Bill asked the obvious question.

"Isn't that our hoody...?"

Chapter 7

September 2022.

Bill, now homeless, went to the local shops to buy some clothes and essential toiletries to enable him to continue a semi-normal life from the company flat. It is now two weeks from the time he met up with Wally and he decided to give him a ring for an up-date. Returning to the flat he quick-dialled Wally's number.

"Hiya, Wally. Any news on the fire?"

"Nothing formal, but the Fire Officer tells me that his report is on its way to me. I'll give you a bell when it arrives, and we'll look at it together."

"Okay. Any update on hoody?"

"Nah, nothing yet, but we're still on the case. We're not going to have much joy until we get a good look at his face. I'll prod Jim about it and let you know."

"Great. Thanks."

Bill laid his mobile on the bed next to him while he pondered his next move. There was a knock on the flat door. Opening this, he smiled to see Elle stood there.

"Hi, dad. Have you had breakfast yet?"

"Not yet. Do you want to go get some?"

"Sure thing."

Letting Brad know they were leaving the office they made their way to the nearby cafe. After ordering breakfast they sat chatting while their order was prepared and delivered.

Elle asked Bill, "Have you heard from the Coroner yet?"

"No. I thought I would give him a prod by email some time. What about you?"

"Nope. Nothing. They've probably got a lot on, especially after that multicar pile-up on the North Circular yesterday."

"Yeah. Perhaps I'll wait for a while. They might have something to give me next week."

Elle asked, "Have you heard from Wally?"

"Spoke recently. I don't want to disturb him too much, he's a busy bloke."

"Any thoughts on when you're coming back to work?"

"I reckon I'll be ready on Monday. That gives me the weekend to go look at this field that I've inherited. It'll give me a day away from all this."

"Good idea, dad. I'll let Brad know."

The following morning Bill signed out the company car and travelled to Essex. His sat-nav took him all the way to the village of Colbert while he relaxed and considered all that had happened recently.

He still grieved for Amy but being pragmatic, he accepted that time heals, and he had decided that it was time to get back into the swing of things. Although he couldn't help worrying if Elle had, by now, accepted the situation. She seemed up-beat when they last met, but who knows what she may be suppressing under her cheerful, devil-may-care approach to life?

He found Colbert village to be locked in a time capsule. Nothing appeared to have changed since it was built in the 1700s. It had quaint two-up, two-down cottages surrounded by rose gardens divided by paths leading to the low cottage doors. Each building was topped with a thatched roof and tiny chimney allowing wisps of smoke to escape into the autumn sky.

The cottages and shops in this pretty, picturesque chocolate box village were separated by a cobbled road that vibrated the steering wheel on Bill's car as he searched for a place to park.

As he stood on the ancient, paved footpath, stretching from the tedious journey, he had a vision of horses pulling carts of merchandise clattering along the street. He imagined tiny stalls lining the road, each one laden with fruit and vegetables harvested from the nearby fields.

Seeing a charming little tea house, he decided that this was the place to begin his search for Colbert's Field. Sitting at one of the few tables in the tea house he ordered a pot of tea and cream bun and watched the world go by through the tiny cottage window.

The waitress put the tray on his table and asked, "Can I get you anything else?"

"No, thank you. This is fine. Is it always this busy in here?" looking round the room at the four empty tables with a smile.

"Although we're a bit out of the way here we get a good trade in passing visitors, like you," laughed the waitress. "Are you here for long?"

Bill couldn't help wondering if she was flirting with him. She looked to be somewhere in her mid-30s.

"No. I've just come to look at Colbert's Field," volunteered Bill. "Can you give me some directions?"

"Of course," the waitress smiled and sat down opposite Bill. "It's easy. You go out of the village in that direction," pointing, "until you get to the cross-roads. Turn right and Colbert's Field is about half-a-mile on the right. The bridge over the stream is right next to the corner of the field. From there you'll be able to get access. You'll have to climb over the big, padlocked gate because it's private property and it's surrounded on three sides by a dry-stone wall. Been like that for over twenty years."

"Sounds like you know the area pretty well?"

"We used to swim in the stream when we were kids," she laughed," and we swam under the bridge and took boys up onto the field because it was so private behind the wall to… You know… Do what our parents told us not to do."

"Ahh, memories," smiled Bill. "I remember those times. Great fun, eh?"

"Absolutely. Memories are a bit distant, now, though."

"Yeah. Know what you mean."

With that, Bill stood up and dropped a twenty-pound note on the table.

"I'll just get your change," the woman said.

"Nah. Keep the change," dismissed Bill. He asked, "You got a name?"

"Melissa… Mel… Are you the gentleman that owns the field?" asked the waitress.

"I do now, Mel. Only just heard that I inherited it."

"You're not going to build a load of houses on it, are you. It would be a shame to spoil that field with an ugly estate. It's lovely county-side."

"I doubt it. I don't really know what I'm going to do with it. I've not even seen it, yet."

"Don't spoil it," pleaded the woman.

Bill smiled at her and left the tea house to find his car. On the way to the car, he wondered why Mel was so adamant that the field should not be developed. "Mind you," he said to himself, looking back at Mel watching him from her doorway, "It is beautiful around here."

He found a convenient lay-by about ten yards from the bridge.

As he walked down the road he had to stop and make way for a rust bucket of a pick-up truck heading towards him. The driver slowed as he passed by, and Bill felt the hairs on his neck stand to attention as the driver of the pick-up glared an evil eye at him through the truck window. Although the look on the truck driver's face unnerved Bill he ignored it and carried on towards the gate. Taking a quick look over his shoulder he saw the truck at a standstill next to Bill's car, its engine spewing out exhaust from its tail-pipe. Bill turned and stood looking at the truck for a few seconds before it took off in the direction of Colbert Village.

Surprisingly, he found the gate very slightly ajar when he approached it, despite the waitress's words that it was pad-locked. There was no chain or padlock.

Leaning into the gate to push it open its rusty hinges screeched as they complained about being disturbed. Bill entered the field and was met by a sight that he never expected to see.

From his vantage point he could see a manor house proudly standing in front of five picture-postcard cottages.

"This can't be right," he thought. "Nobody said anything about there being all this stuff on the field."

He didn't go any further, thinking that perhaps he had trespassed onto the wrong field. Instead, he followed the dry-stone wall all the way round its perimeter with his eyes. He didn't see any entry point other than the rusty old iron gate.

"But that gate's not been opened for years," he thought, puzzled at the pristine condition of the cottages and manor house. How did the occupants get onto the field to go to their cottages… And who lives in that manor house?

He decided to make further enquiries with Symonds, Baker & Stace as he turned and headed back to his car.

Chapter 8

Back at the flat, Bill relaxed until the following Monday. He knew that the solicitor's office would be closed for the weekend, so he pottered around doing some housework and surfing the Internet. It was a good time to catch up on a few zeds before returning to work.

Having handed in the company car, he shared the lift up to the office floor with a few of his employees. They all sympathised with the loss of Amy and welcomed him back to the office.

Brad warmly welcomed Bill back with a man hug. They sat in Brad's office to catch up with work stuff. Brad explained what had happened about the missing Belgium stamps and other mundane work stuff, then relaxed in the plush chairs.

"Have you heard from Wally, yet?" asked Brad.

"No, I'll tackle him today."

"What about the fire? Had the fire report, yet?"

"Nope. I'm leaving that alone until Wally's had a chance to see it."

"Okay. Keep me in the loop?"

"Of course."

Bill stood to leave Brad's office.

"Take it easy," Brad smiled.

Bill said his hellos to Julie on the way to his office. She gave him a hug and a broad smile.

"Great to see you back," she said, then her smile faded as she gave him an update on the one and only call that he had missed during his absence.

"I got a call from David March, the other day, asking when you'll be calling in to clear Amy's office out," she advised. "Do you want me to arrange someone to do that for you?"

"No, it's okay. I'll give him a ring back today and arrange a visit."

"Coffee?" asked Julie.

"Best offer I've had all morning…" smiled Bill as he entered his office.

He didn't really feel like sorting through Amy's stuff, yet, but it had to be done and it wasn't fair to David to keep his office space occupied for no reason.

He phoned Nigel Stace, the solicitor. Stace's secretary advised that Nigel was, "… in court all this week," so a provisional appointment was made for Wednesday, next week.

His next call was to Elle's office, just round the corner from his own.

"Fancy some lunch?" asked Bill.

"Can't," she replied. "I'm off to meet our Internet team to discuss an update for our web pages. How about dinner, tonight?"

"Great. Your place at seven?"

"It's a date."

Replacing the handset, Bill sat back and reflected on how much he missed Amy. With a resigned sigh he dialled Wally's number.

"Hi Wally. It's Bill."

"Oh, hello Bill. I was just about to call you with a progress report."

"Shoot," invited Bill, feeling a little more upbeat that Wally might have some news.

"I've got the fire report in front of me," informed Wally. "I'll send you a copy."

"No, don't do that. I can come round to your place to pick it up. It'll be quicker."

"Okay. Later this morning then?"

"Perfect."

Bill stood up and went to Julie's desk.

"Can you telephone David March to arrange a meeting for Thursday this week?"

"Of course," replied Julie.

Bill continued, "Can you then call Nigel Stace's secretary to confirm my meeting for Wednesday, next week? I told her I would call back when I'd had a chance to look at my diary. Don't forget to diary both appointments."

"Will do. Going out?"

"Yeah. I thought I'd get a bit of brunch, then go on to Wally's office to read the Fire report. Can you let Brad know?"

"Yep. See you later this afternoon?"

"Yep."

Finishing his brunch, Bill hailed a taxi to take him to Wally's office.

On arrival he was greeted with a firm handshake by Wally and ushered into the office. Wally invited him to sit and went round to his side of the desk to retrieve the fire report from his in-tray. Wally's secretary had followed the men into the office, carrying a tray of coffee and biscuits. Wally sat next to Bill on the couch and munched on the biscuits while Bill read and digested the report.

With a sigh Bill looked at Wally and angrily asserted, "There is no way that fire was an accident," he declared in frustration.

Wally tried to pacify Bill. "They made a thorough investigation, Bill. They took the place apart... The rubble anyway. They didn't miss a thing."

"I accept that," said Bill. "I'm not criticising the report, but I find it really hard to accept that they conclude that the gas explosion was '...*caused by an unidentified incident,*' reading from the report.

"I spoke to the Fire Officer this morning, just before you arrived," replied Wally. "The fire had obliterated any evidence that may have been available. With no evidence to prove otherwise the only conclusion that anyone can make is that it was an accident."

"Well, I'm not convinced, Wally. We've both been to house fires in the past. When have you ever seen one as fierce as this one? It says here that the fire investigator found traces of accelerant?"

"Yeah, but not enough to firmly state that was the cause of so much damage."

Bill looked at the report dejectedly.

"Have you got any more on hoody?"

"Our guys have done what they can with both the video from your place and the neighbour's video. It's impossible to see his face. We're going to have to close that line of enquiry down."

Feeling as low as he had ever felt, Bill left Wally's office.

The fire department are closing their file, the police are closing their file, and on the surface of it people seem to believe that Amy's death was an accident.

Not so, in Bill's mind.

Bill filled in the rest of the afternoon with mundane report checking in the office. After a brief chat with Brad about the fire report he went to the flat to shower and get changed for Elle's dinner party.

He turned up at Elle's place a polite five minutes early and was welcomed with hugs and kisses by both Elle and

Janice. The girls' boyfriends were chatting in the lounge, each waving a glass of wine as they chatted. Introductions over, everyone sat round the dining table and eagerly awaited the tureen of soup that Janice had prepared for their first course.

The evening went smoothly, everyone chatting, joking and taking the mickey out of each other. They played a couple of party games before the boys eventually bid the remainder farewell and left the flat to go find a late-open pub. Janice made her excuses and went to bed, leaving Elle and Bill in the lounge, finishing the dregs of wine.

They discussed the fire report and its ramifications of accepting that the fire was an accident. Elle didn't appear to be too upset by the findings.

"How you holding up?" asked Bill.

"I'm fine," Elle responded. "How about you?"

"I'm over it, now, but I still miss her terribly."

Elle paused while she thought about how she was going to tell Bill what she wanted to get off her chest.

"Dad, I have to tell you something about mum but you're not going to like what I say. I really don't know how to tell you."

"Just come right out and say it, Elle. I'm a big boy now, you, know."

"… I think mum was having an affair."

Bill scrutinised Elle's face and saw that she was serious.

Calmly, he asked, "What makes you think that?"

Elle shuffled next to him, clearly embarrassed.

"I… I… I'm sure. Haven't you noticed any changes in her, lately? I have."

"Elle, you can't say that mum's having an affair just because you think you've seen a couple of changes in her."

"You've not answered the question, Dad. Have you seen any changes?" Tears were beginning to well in Elle's eyes.

"No, I haven't," replied Bill with some exasperation. "What changes?"

Elle composed herself, unwrapped herself from inside Bill's arms and sat back with a resigned look.

"Dad," she said with a hint of anger, "You've put Mum on a pedestal and worshipped her since you were married. You're blind to what's been going on in front of you. I know how much you loved Mum. I loved her as well, but she wasn't the angel you made her out to be. Why can't you accept that her perfection was marred by an affair?"

Tears began to roll down Elle's cheeks.

Bill had heard as much as he wanted to hear and anyway, he didn't want to see Elle lose any more of her temper. He stood up to leave.

"That's right," Elle shouted, "Run away. They say that the truth is hardest to take from someone close to you."

"I'm not running," Bill replied calmly, "I'm just going to put the kettle on. Looks like you need a cup of coffee to sober you up."

With that he went to the kitchen instead of leaving and he reflected on what Elle had just disclosed. She was so sure about Amy's affair and Bill really didn't want to know about it. Why should he spoil years of blissful marriage with gossip? He didn't think Elle had any right to force it on him, but he supposed he should listen to what she had to say, if only to let her get it off her chest.

He sat down beside her, once more, and put her hot drink on the coffee table in front of them.

"Right now, I don't really care what she did when she wasn't with me. She cared enough to make me feel good, and loved, and wanted, so it doesn't really matter about anything else now that she is dead."

"You're right," sobbed Elle, "I'm sorry, Dad. I didn't mean to lose my temper. I didn't want an argument. I just thought you should know, that's all."

"Okay, tell me what you want to tell me, then we can both put it behind us."

Elle described how, last year, she was travelling back to the office from the Internet team's hub, and she saw Amy on the concourse of Waterloo station kissing another man. At first, she refused to believe it was Amy and thought that, perhaps, she had been mistaken.

A couple of months later she again saw the same couple in front of platform eleven greeting each other with kisses and hugs, arms wrapped around each other in a loving embrace. Elle changed her position so as to get a better look at the couple. There was no mistaking Amy's happiness as he greeted the man in front of her.

On the next occasion Elle had decided to follow the couple to see what happened. They exited the station and walked, arm-in-arm, down to the nearest hotel. Elle watched from the entrance door as the man booked them into the hotel, and they both then disappeared towards the hotel lifts.

"Did you recognise the bloke?" asked Bill.

"No, I couldn't get a clear look at his face. He had his back to me all the time and I didn't want to make it known that I'd followed Mum. I'm sure I've seen him before, though."

Bill reflected on Elle's account of what she saw and decided that perhaps it was time to let sleeping dogs lie.

There is a lot of sense in the old adage that *'What the eye don't see, the heart can't grieve about'*.

Chapter 9

As arranged by Julie, Bill attended the office of Globe Publications on the Thursday morning. The guard on the security desk buzzed him through the turnstile, signed him in, issued him with a visitor badge and gave him directions to David March's office.

Bill entered the lift in front of several Globe employees eagerly jostling to start work. Many of them departed from the lift before Bill arrived at his chosen floor and when the lift door slid open, he followed the remaining workers out, accidentally brushing shoulders with Hugo.

"Sorry," Bill offered, but no response was forthcoming. Bill just continued walking towards David's office without looking back. He didn't see Hugo glaring at him from the lift.

Susan, David's secretary, ushered Bill into David's office. The two men greeted each other, and David offered Bill sincere condolences. David asked Susan to bring in some coffee and invited Bill to take a seat in a comfortable buttoned couch facing the desk.

While the two men chatted, Bill studied David.

Promoted in 1999 to CEO of Globe Publications David was every inch a publicist, with a smart three-piece suit, shiny shoes, manicured nails and a good head of salt and pepper coloured hair. For his age he was in good shape and clearly had a gym subscription somewhere close to the office. Bill didn't know if he was married, but he would certainly be a steal for any woman looking for a mate. For a split second, Bill thought back to Elle's outburst about

Amy's affair, but the thought was gone as quickly as it had appeared.

"Amy was our best Editor," stated David. "We were all sorry to hear what happened. She will be sorely missed by us...Truly, a sad loss."

"She was best at the things she liked," reminisced Bill. "I'm sure she will be missed by a lot of people. She never had a bad word to say about anyone."

"That's true. One of her most endearing qualities." David was genuinely sad in his reflections of Amy.

The coffee arrived. Susan placed the tray on the low table in front of Bill and began to pour the coffee.

David asked her, "Susan, can you ask Hugo to spare us a moment?" Turning to Bill he said, "I thought I'd ask him to show you to Amy's office."

Susan replied to David, "He's just popped down to the amender's office for a moment to discuss the changes to the Brown's Catalogue. He shouldn't be too long." The latter statement was addressed to Bill.

"No probs," declared Bill.

Bill and David sat chewing the fat while they drank their coffee. After about ten minutes there was a tap on the door which was opened by Susan. Hugo brushed passed her and approached David.

"You wanted to see me, David?" he asked.

"Yes. This is Bill Colbert, Amy's husband," introduced David. Bill stood and took Hugo's hand. He immediately recognised Hugo as the bloke he had brushed shoulders with, at the lift, but Bill kept a straight-laced face, not wanting to let on that he recognised him.

"Sorry about Amy," Hugo offered. "She was a good friend."

Bill smiled and nodded to Hugo in agreement.

David asked Hugo to take Bill to Amy's office so that he could pick up her belongings.

Turning to Bill, Hugo said, "I've already packed her stuff into a box for you, Bill. Follow me?"

With that Bill gave his thanks to David, said his farewell and followed Hugo out of the office. As the two men walked along Globe's corridors, they passed the time of day by chatting about Amy.

Hugo was taller than Bill, swarthy looking with a shock of dark hair that was obviously silver under the Grecian 2000 dye. Bill silently noted that his roots needed doing again, clearly an indication of Hugo's age and possible narcissistic traits. He sported a walrus moustache that any Victorian explorer would be proud of.

He explained how he and Amy had frequently discussed work in the firm's canteen during lunch hour, and with a touch of sadness in his voice he declared how much Amy will be missed by him. She was, according to Hugo, his shoulder to lean on when David criticised his work, and Amy always had new ideas to pass on to him about his work.

Hugo asked Bill how Elle had taken Amy's death. This question unnerved Bill slightly. Hugo's familiarity with Amy showed that they clearly had a bond, but Bill put this down to a working relationship more than anything else and thought nothing more of it.

"She'll be okay," answered Bill. "How long you worked here?"

"Oh, since about 2019," volunteered Hugo. "About the same time as Amy joined us here at the office to work full time," he reminisced.

Hugo left Bill at the door to Amy's office after introducing Bill to Isobel, Amy's former secretary. Isobel also offered her condolences and talked of good things about Amy. Bill entered the office and looked around.

He'd never had an opportunity to visit Amy's office after her promotion, although he had attended the Christmas and celebration parties held by the firm on occasion. Despite having been introduced to various people in the firm he had quickly forgotten about them. David, Amy's boss, didn't even register with him when they were introduced by David's secretary.

Looking round, Bill was impressed by the advances that Amy had made in her working life. The office was equally as large as David's office and had a commanding view of the London skyline.

With a touch of sadness, he turned to the cardboard box containing Amy's possessions, sitting on the desk. Inside was her business handbag and lots of articles that one collects and displays in one's office. He opened the handbag to see the usual tissues and trinkets that women secret away in their handbags, together with her mobile phone. He would look at the phone later. Perhaps it will hold some clues about the fire. Under her handbag was a picture frame with a photo of Bill and Amy in some distant restaurant, squashing together for the benefit of the camera, in front of a table displaying a cake with a single burning candle on top.

Bill remembered this picture being taken. It was when they had stayed in a plush hotel in Bermuda on their first wedding anniversary. Bill chuckled as he remembered asking a passing bloke to take the photo, but the bloke merely passed the camera to a little boy holding his hand. The boy had taken a good picture…

His thoughts were abruptly brought back to the present as he noted that the glass on the picture frame was cracked. It wasn't like Amy to display damaged goods and she invariably put right what needed putting right immediately the damage was sustained. She wouldn't have tolerated displaying such an injured photo frame, especially with a photo of herself and Bill on show. *'Perhaps the glass got damaged while it was being packed?'* thought Bill, putting his thoughts behind him.

Isobel entered the office as Bill was about to return the picture frame back to the box.

"The glass was broken when I picked it out of the bin," she advised.

"The bin?" questioned Bill. "This bin?" pointing to the waste bin sat next to the desk.

"Yes. I thought it best to let you decide if you wanted it."

"That was kind of you. Yes, I do want to keep it. I'll get it re-framed."

Bill left Globe's offices with Amy's box of possessions and hailed a taxi to take him back to his own office. Who had thrown the photo frame in the bin, and why? Perhaps it was because the glass was broken?

Whatever the reason, the thought sat uncomfortably in Bill's mind as the taxi meandered through the London traffic.

Chapter 10

The following week Bill visited the solicitor's office, as previously arranged.

He was, once more, greeted by the neat receptionist with her paper-white, friendly smile.

"God morning, Mr. Colbert."

Bill was flattered that she remembered him from their last encounter.

"Good morning. I've got an appointment with Mr. Stace."

"Oh, I'm terribly sorry. Mr. Stace is off sick presently." She consulted the diary in front of her. "We've switched your appointment to meet our Mr. Baker, Mr. Stace's Partner."

Bill was offered the obligatory coffee and he made himself comfortable on the plush couch while the secretary telephoned Mr. Baker. After about ten minutes a door to the reception was opened and another Victorian look-alike poked his head into reception.

"Mr. Colbert? Would you care to come into my office?"

Bill followed Baker into his office and was bid to sit on yet another Victorian buttoned easy chair.

"What can we do for you?" enquired Baker.

Bill had brought with him the envelope containing the inheritance documents and the bulky key.

"It's about this field I've inherited."

Baker rummaged through the files on his desk but was frustrated to find that Bill's file wasn't there. He excused himself, opened his door and asked the receptionist for

Bill's file. A couple of embarrassing silent minutes later she reappeared with the file and handed it to Baker, apologising for not handing it to Baker earlier. Baker opened the file and studied its contents.

"Yes, how can I be of service?"

"Well," Bill continued, "when I met with Nigel Stace, he never mentioned any buildings on the site. I'd assumed it was an empty field."

"Oh? I'm surprised they were not mentioned."

Baker wrote something on a yellow post-it note, removed the note from its pad and went to his door once more. Opening this he poked his head outside and handed the note to the receptionist.

"Will you put a call in to the archive office and ask them to look up any information about this reference number and get it to me asap?"

"Of course," replied the receptionist. Shall I bring in some coffee?"

Baker relocated his head back into the office and asked Bill, "Coffee?"

"Great, thanks," acknowledged Bill.

The solicitor returned to his desk.

"I'm sorry about this Mr. Colbert. The file will take just a few minutes to get here…I'm a little annoyed that Nigel hadn't collated ALL information prior to meeting you."

"No need for an apology. Mistakes get made."

The two men sat chatting about the inheritance while waiting for the missing file. Bill opened his envelope and extracted its contents to show Baker. The solicitor read the documents and then picked up the key to inspect it closely.

"That's interesting."

He put the key back on the coffee table and went to retrieve his own file from his desk. Reading the contents of this he looked puzzled and said, more to himself than anyone else, "I wonder what that is all about?"

After several minutes there was another light knock on the door and the receptionist entered with another file. The solicitor spread this on his desk and studied its contents.

Picking up a photograph he turned to Bill and asked, "What kind of buildings are on the field?"

"What seems to be a manor house of some kind and a few cottages," explained Bill.

The solicitor came round his desk to give Bill the photograph.

"Anything like these buildings?" he asked.

Bill studied the photo. It was an extremely grainy sepia photo, seemingly taken from where Bill had stood when he went to see the field for himself. The fuzzy image showed the side of the manor house with a couple of the cottages also in the shot. Turning the photo over he noted a date of 1900 handwritten on the back.

"They certainly look like the buildings I saw," offered Bill.

He looked up at Baker, who was still studying the documents in front of him. Baker had extracted Bill's file from the coffee table, and he was comparing this with the one recently brought in. After a while he spoke up.

"Well, although there is no mention of any buildings on this site, the will made out by Willum Colbert in1736 clearly states '… *the field and everything within its boundary walls.*' On this basis it would appear that the buildings belong to you. This key may be the key to the manor house. Sometimes, these manors were hidden behind gates that needed a key to unlock them."

Baker inspected the key further. "It doesn't look as if that key has been used for a long time. Would you like me to conduct further enquiries on your behalf?"

"No, thanks. I'll look into it myself. Can I keep this photo?"

"Of course. It's yours. You do realise that there may be quite a tidy sum of rent accrued, from the cottages. Do you wish us to look into that aspect for you?"

"No, it's okay. I'm not interested in making waves along those lines. If people have lived rent free for God knows how long they can keep what is owed. I'll not bother them now."

"That's very generous of you, Mr. Colbert. You seem to have inherited some of your ancestor's good will."

"Yeah well, I've managed without the money 'till now. I'm sure I can survive without it from here on."

Bill collated all his documents back into his folder, bid the solicitor goodbye and returned to his office.

Scrutinising the photo on his way out of the office, he was still puzzled as to why Stace had not looked into the matter of the buildings more thoroughly.

Chapter 11

November 2022.

Six weeks had passed since Bill's meeting with the solicitor. He'd had no chance to re-visit Colbert's Field since then because work commitments had kept him busy. Meeting with Brad, one morning, they discussed their workload in relation to a forthcoming important event. An event that was too far down the road to cancel or ignore.

Their Facilities Manager had persuaded the two Partners to get the office re-wired, re-decorated and re-furnished. He put up a good argument to bring the firm into the twenty-first century with upgraded furniture and equipment. After submitting the appropriate spreadsheet confirming that the firm could afford such measures Bill and Brad had many discussions, and many staff meetings, about the proposal and had eventually agreed to go ahead with the refurbishment. The FM had approached the landlord to discuss matters, had been given approval and had arranged the works to start on the eighth of this month. It will take five weeks for the works to be completed.

Such an upheaval would necessitate having to re-locate to temporary offices, but the landlord had generously offered a spare floor in the same building for a fraction of the rent. Unfortunately, the temporary office didn't have an integral flat, so Bill had to find somewhere else to crash while the works were being carried out.

Bill and Elle had several conversations about this predicament and Elle had kindly offered her couch for Bill to crash, but he didn't feel that he could impose so much on her, and he graciously declined the invitation.

He was tempted to ask Julie to arrange a room in one of the nearby hotels, but he suddenly had a flash of inspiration. He owned a manor house!

He asked Julie to research the nearest rail stations to Colbert Village, and the rail times from those stations. Good fortune was on his side as he learned that there was a good rail service from Seven Kings rail station, about a fifteen-minute drive from Colbert Village. There was also a convenient car park at the station. The whole journey from the manor house would take just over an hour and a half, but he would work from the manor and only travel to the office if necessary. He could use the Internet connection on his phone, but he decided to wait until he got there to see what facilities he needed. If absolutely necessary he could always get the firm's FM to set him up from a convenient room inside the manor… Assuming, of course that there was one.

On his way out of the office he poked his head round Elle's doorway and let her know what his plans were. He did the same with Brad, then collected his things from the flat and headed towards the car park. He would travel to Colbert's Field today to take a much closer look at his inheritance.

It was early afternoon when Bill arrived at Colbert Village. He decided to have a brunch at the tea house; it will be a good opportunity to get to know the attractive Mel a bit better. Perhaps she could come for tea at his place, some time…

Mel's broad smile greeted him as soon as he entered the tea house.

"Back again? Can't stay away from me, eh?"

She was definitely flirting, this time.

"Couldn't resist your smile… And some of that delicious steak pie," he flirted back.

"Take a seat and I'll bring it in a moment."

Bill admired her shapely legs and trim figure as she returned to the kitchen. He couldn't help wondering if she had a partner tucked away somewhere.

After about ten minutes she returned to the table carrying a tray full of crockery and a steaming steak pie. Placing this on the table in front of Bill she turned to go back to the kitchen.

"Don't go," Bill said. She turned to face him. "Sit down and have a chat while I munch my way through this pie… Unless you're too busy serving this multitude of customers," he joked, looking round at the empty room.

Mel smiled a bright 'come on' smile and sat opposite him. "What brings you back to this metropolis of excitement, then?" she prompted.

In between mouthfuls of pie Bill waved his fork around and replied, "Seeing as how I've inherited a vast swathe of this countryside, I thought I'd take a better look at it."

"Good for you. You're not thinking of building on it, are you?" asked Mel with a concerned look on her face.

Bill recollected that she had asked this the last time he visited.

He chuckled, "No, of course not, although I'll be taking a closer look at the manor."

"That old thing. It needs more than a look. It needs pulling down." laughed Mel.

He was more than a bit perplexed at this comment. He saw the manor last time he visited the field and there was no way that such a grand building should be *'pulled down.'*

He didn't press the point but instead decided to change the subject.

"I'm surprised this place makes enough to stay alive," he said, looking round.

"Well, there's no mortgage and I get quite a lot of passing trade. I earn enough to pay the bills and keep the kitchen ticking over and I live over the top of the shop, so I don't have far to come to work. It's quiet, it's convenient and it's mine."

"Oops! I was expecting a grey-haired old lady sat somewhere in the back room, counting her takings and underpaying the staff. Didn't realise you owned the place; you look too young." Bill was blushing from ear to ear.

Mel laughed as she collected the dishes to take back to the kitchen. "You're not the only one to inherit something, you know. I inherited this place a couple of years ago." She sat down again and smiled at Bill. "It was originally a cottage, like the rest of them on this road, but I decided to convert it to what it is today. It's not much, but like I said, it's mine… I'll be back in a minute."

She took the tray full of used dishes back to the kitchen and returned with a pot of coffee. They both enjoyed each other's company as they drank their coffee. When the coffee was finished Bill looked at his watch and told Mel that it was time for him to leave.

"The gate to the field needs a bit of work doing on it. Do you know any builders around here that would be willing to look at it for me? I can't open it far enough to get the car into the field."

"That'll be old George. He's more of an odd-job man than he is a builder, but his work is good and I'm sure you'll be pleased with him. I can give him a call now, if you like."

"Great. Thanks. Can you ask him to meet me at the gates?"

"Of course. When you meet him ignore his manners. He's a grumpy old sod at the best of times, but his heart is in the right place."

With that, Mel went to the cash till, picked up the telephone receiver and dialled George's number. When he answered she asked him to meet Bill at the gates and to also fix the gates so that Bill could drive his car through. Replacing the handset, she told Bill that George would be at the gates in ten minutes.

Bill thanked her and left the tea house. On the way to his car, he realised that he had not paid for his meal. Chastising himself for this omission he quickly turned and headed back to the tea house.

Entering, he called out for Mel who poked her head round the kitchen doorway.

"I forgot to pay," said Bill, with some embarrassment.

"Don't worry. Pay me next time you come," she smiled.

A thought flashed into his head but disappeared as quickly as it had emerged. "There was a definite connection between Mel and himself…"

He promised Mel that he would return for more of her delicious cooking, a promise she demanded he keep.

Bill had already borrowed some bedding from Elle so that he could sleep in the flat. He had brought this with him.

After visiting a quaint corner shop, to buy some food supplies for his stay at the manor, Bill drove to the gates.

Chapter 12

Arriving at the lay-by, in front of the gates, Bill saw the rust bucket pick-up truck parked in front of the gates. George, the driver with the evil eye, was at the top of a ladder clearing weeds and old dead branches from the tops of the gates. Seeing Bill arrive, he climbed down the ladder and the two men approached each other, hands outstretched for their handshake.

"Want some help?" asked Bill.

"You the gent that wants these 'ere gates fixed?"

"Yeah. Can you fix them so that I can get the car into the field?"

"All's needed is a bit of grease on them 'inges. Got some in the truck. You clear the rubbish away from the gates and I'll go get my strimmer to cut down the grass. Chuck that rubbish in the back of the truck," instructed George as he trundled towards the rust bucket.

Bill heard him mutter something like, "Bloody city folk coming 'ere and upsetting things!"

Bill wasn't exactly dressed for this type of manual labour, neither was he used to it. Nonetheless, he showed willing by removing his jacket and getting stuck into the rubbish removal. Some inconsiderate lout had fly-tipped a mattress and some broken furniture and debris in front of the gates and behind them there was a pile of black plastic bags full of garbage and old clothes.

About an hour later, the rubbish had been cleared, the hinges greased, the grass cut, and the gates opened, this time without screeching in anger. Bill was impressed with

George's work, and he asked how much did he want for the work.

"You pay me what you think it was worth," declared George." If I think it's not enough, you won't get any more work from me in the future."

After putting his jacket back on, Bill took out a fifty-pound note from his wallet and offered it to George.

"Where d'yer think I'm goin' to get that thing changed around 'ere?" he questioned with some belligerence.

Bill thought about this conundrum and came up with a suggestion.

"Tell you what. I'll give this to Mel at the tea shop. She can probably change it for you. Any good?"

"It'll do, I suppose," grumbled George. "Mind you don't forget, now," he demanded.

"I won't."

"Why do you want to drive into that field anyway? It's not been touched for years."

"Because it's there…" answered Bill.

George gave Bill a puzzled look, as if Bill was an idiot. He obviously didn't see the sardonic side of Bill's reply, so he collected up his tools, threw them on top of the rubbish in the back of his pickup and drove away, spewing out a black cloud of exhaust fumes from the back of the truck.

As Bill watched George disappear into the distance, he couldn't help wondering what George had meant by, "… It's not been touched for years."

"Perhaps he's talking about not having the grass cut?" thought Bill.

He reflected on his last visit to the field…When he had admired the pristine condition of the cottages. "Perhaps," he thought, "they just squeezed between the partially opened gates to get in and out of the field?"

This thought satisfied his curiosity on the questions at the back of his mind, and he shrugged in acceptance.

He drove up to the manor thinking that quite a lot of work is needed to make the original driveway user friendly once more. The car bounced up and down on its springs, sometimes scraping the oil sump on the ground.

Arriving in front of the manor he retrieved the solicitor's large envelope from his briefcase and tipped the key onto the adjacent car seat. Exiting the car and standing against it with his arms resting on its roof he looked at the manor's large oak door with a porch light hanging above the covered entrance. He was surprised that the manor didn't seem to have been vandalised in any way. No broken windows, no graffiti, no rubbish strewn around. Thinking how unusual this was, especially in view of the lengthy period that the manor had laid dormant, he turned to look at the cottages.

Five cottages…Five pretty postcard picture cottages with neatly manicured thatched roofs, tiny chimneys poking out of the thatch. Five identical cottages with two up, two down rooms and pretty rose gardens divided by well-worn paths. Just like the village. Five cottages with tiny leadlight windows surrounded by neatly pruned climbing roses that ascend from the gardens. Each cottage facing the manor in humble deference.

Bill noticed that each cottage was named after the type of rose surrounding those windows;

Iceberg Rose Cottage,
Pilgrim Rose Cottage,
Gloriana Rose Cottage,
Sunrise Rose Cottage, and
Alaska Rose Cottage.

What centuries old secrets were hiding behind those windows? Secrets that never escaped from the pretty cottages. Secrets never to be told.

As Bill turned back to admire the manor, he thought he saw a movement in one of the upstairs windows. It looked like someone had ducked behind the curtains. Perhaps he just saw a shadow. Perhaps he imagined it. With a shrug of his shoulders, he went to open the large oak door.

Despite its age, the key turned easily in the lock, as if the lock had just been oiled. He didn't give this much thought, his mind trying to picture what he would find when he opened the door.

The vestibule behind the door was everything he imagined an eighteenth-century vestibule would be. Oak panelling surrounding a grand staircase to the upper floors in the centre, with heavy oak doors leading to the various ground floor rooms. Which one should he choose to open first? The one tucked against the wall at the rear of the staircase, or the one to his right, or maybe the one to his left?

He surmised that ones to his left and right opened to reception rooms. "Let's have a look at the kitchen, first," he said to himself, thinking that it would soon be time for something to eat.

He was right about where this led to. The odd thing about the kitchen, though, was that it was not as dirty or dusty as he imagined it would be. Just a thin layer of dust covered everything, from the oak worktops to the pans hanging from a frame suspended from the ceiling. The cupboards were typical Victorian style farmhouse cupboards. A proud Aga stood opposite a tall fireplace on the floor of which was a rusty grate, still with the remnants of some long ago log fire. A heavy oak kitchen table occupied the centre of the room. Bill imagined this being covered with all sorts of vegetables being prepared for a long-forgotten dinner, with a stern cook giving orders to the maids who served the meal.

Bill opened a couple of drawers to see what was inside. Much as expected, there was nothing but shrivelled grease-proof paper lining the bottoms of the drawers. In one drawer, however, he found a bunch of large keys…The type of keys that fit mortice locks. He replaced these keys back in the drawer, intending to find out what doors they fitted, later.

He returned to the car to retrieve the bedding and other chattels. Arms loaded, he headed back towards the manor. Again, he thought he saw a movement in the same upstairs window, out of the corner of his eye. With an abrupt stop he stared at the window for some time before deciding that his mind was playing tricks with him.

Dumping the contents of his car boot on the floor of the vestibule he went back outside to find some firewood for the Aga. Around the back of the manor, he found a covered wood store half full of logs that had, at some time in the past, been chopped and piled ready to use. The logs, by now were bone dry, as would be expected, and he carried a huge armful back to the kitchen. He would find the key that fits the rear kitchen door, sometime, but he had better things to do right now. Like getting the Aga up and running and exploring the rest of the manor while the kettle boiled.

Back in the kitchen he turned on one of the taps. Dirty brown water trickled out of the tap, at first, then gushed out of the pipe. Bill decided to leave the tap running to flush out the centuries of dirt in the pipes while he explored upstairs.

He felt quietly awe-inspired as he climbed the luxurious staircase with polished marble bannisters on ornate balustrades. The stair carpet had long ago perished but he could still make out the lush colours that adorned the stairs.

On the landing he was, again, met with oak panelling and five heavy oak doors hiding the rooms behind them. All the doors were locked so he dashed down the stairs to retrieve the keys that he found in the kitchen drawer. Choosing the door to the room he thought he saw some movement from he tried several keys before finding the one that fitted that door.

Gingerly creaking this door back on its hinges, he peered inside the room. It was the master bedroom. Empty, of course, except for the king-size bed occupying the centre of the room. In one corner there was a small wash basin and a door leading from this room opened into a dressing room, decked with clothes racks and shoe cupboards. He went to the large bow window to look at the view. The curtains dropped onto the floor in a bedraggled heap as soon as he tried to open them, dust filling the room. From this window he could see the pretty cottages, some now with wisps of smoke rising from their chimneys. It would appear that someone is at home.

Bill suddenly remembered the running tap in the kitchen. He dashed downstairs and into the kitchen. The tap wasn't running any longer…Looking round the empty kitchen he went over to the sink. The tap had definitely been turned off. He turned the tap back on and found clean water gushing from its spout. He didn't remember turning the tap off, but maybe he did? Perhaps he had turned it off before he went upstairs? Yes, that's it. He had come downstairs to get the door keys and, finding clean water running from the tap, he had turned it off.

"You're letting your imagination run rampant," he chuckled to himself, as he filled the kettle and placed it on the Aga hob.

"Tonight," he said to himself," we'll have a bite to eat, make up that king-sized bed, get an early night and look forward to exploring everywhere tomorrow.

Chapter 13

January 2023.

Office refurbishment had been delayed until the new year. Bill's partner was told the delay was due to sickness and problems with getting materials. Everyone knew it was more to do with the refurbishment firm overbooking jobs, but they were willing to accept penalties and approval was given for them to commence the works on the third of January.

While Bill waited for the refurbishment to be completed, he commuted to the office once each week to drop off and pick up work. He spent his free time exploring the manor and cleaning up the rooms that he stayed in; namely, the front reception (to work in), kitchen, bedroom, changing room, ensuite bathroom, hall, stairs and landing. He intended to tackle the rest as, and when, necessary. Elle had offered to come and help with the clean-up but when Bill refused that offer, she then offered to arrange for a cleaner to attend the property. Again, Bill declined on the basis that he wasn't above a bit of housework and a cleaner, therefore, would be a waste of money.

Elle had been pressing him to let her visit the manor, but Bill declined the request, using the poor state of the place as a suitable excuse. As he had promised to invite her when the place was suitably cleaned up, he decided to get on with the job of dusting and cleaning. He would also need to buy some new curtains because the ones hanging in the bedrooms were falling to pieces.

The things he sorely missed were central heating and running hot water. The central heating aspect was partially overcome with large fires in the fireplace of each of the rooms he occupied. No running hot water, however, was a real pain because he had to heat buckets of water on the Aga and then pour these into a tin bath that he had lugged down from the loft and put in the kitchen. Some time, in the very near future he would arrange to have a proper boiler and immersion tank installed, but this was fairly low on his list of priorities. Before that the electric wiring would need to be upgraded, probably even re-wired.

As long as there was a good supply of logs available, he would, at least, have cooking, hot water and reasonable heating. When necessary, he would ask old George to re-plenish his stock of logs.

Bill settled into his routine of working until early af-ternoon, cleaning until bedtime, bathing and then settling down to read in bed until he was ready for sleep. He was becoming quite the country gentleman.

At the weekends he explored the area surrounding the manor.

Trying not to be intrusive he furtively glanced in each of the downstairs cottage windows to see if anyone was in. Despite not seeing anyone in any of the cottages, wisps of smoke escaped from the chimneys and Bill assumed that all the occupants were in their back rooms, hidden from view. He decided not to knock on any of the doors for fear of dis-turbing his neighbours.

Introductions would be forthcoming soon enough.

Chapter 14

Iceberg Rose Cottage

Late one afternoon, while cleaning his bedroom windows, Bill noticed some movement in one of the cottage windows.

This took him by surprise because he had been for his daily perambulation around the hamlet during the morning and had not seen anyone in any of the cottages. He stared at the cottage window for a while to make sure he wasn't seeing shadows again. Yep, there was definitely a woman in that cottage window… And she was waving to him.

Bill looked at the window cleaning rag in his hand and thought, "I bet she thinks I'm waving to her."

Not wanting to be rude, he dropped the rag in his bucket and waved back. He saw the woman look behind her, then quickly disappear into the dark room. Bill made a mental note to go knock on her door, some time, now that contact had been made. He finished cleaning the window and returned his bucket and rag to the kitchen.

This brief contact piqued Bill's interest in the woman and on each occasion that he visited his bedroom he looked out of the window to see if his neighbour was in view.

Nothing for several days.

Then one afternoon, during his window gazing, the woman came into view once more. She stood in front of her window without moving for a while and Bill was about to wave to her when something horrific happened. His hand froze in mid-air as he saw, to his astonishment, a man grabs the woman's hair from behind her, throw her to the floor and begin kicking her. Bill didn't see the woman once she had been thrown to the floor but watching the man going through the motions left little to his imagination.

In the anger of the moment Bill couldn't make out any of the bully's facial features. Just the back of his head of grey hair. As he angrily turned to pay a visit to this bully, he stopped dead as he saw the woman stand and make her way out of the room.

"At least she's still alive," thought Bill. He watched as the woman painfully exited from the room.

He decided not to make waves. He was concerned that he might make matters worse for the woman and anyway, what goes on in the privacy of someone's home is none of his business. He was, however, anxious about the woman's health and welfare.

The following day Bill ignored his work and his cleaning. He placed a chair at the foot of his bed, facing the window. In the darkness of the room, it will be difficult for anyone to see him looking out of his window and he could sit there for as long as it takes the woman to re-appear at her window. He sat there all through the day and into the night.

At about eight p.m. she re-appeared. Bill sat still for a few seconds to see if the man was prowling around her room. With nothing to suggest that he was anywhere near the woman Bill jumped to his feet, gingerly approached the window and waved. She waved back. A cautious glance behind her confirmed that she was, for the time being, alone.

Using the international language of index finger pointing, Bill pointed in her direction then held up both thumbs in a question of 'You okay?'

She reciprocated by holding up her own thumbs and nodding in the affirmative.

Relieved that she was all right, Bill waved goodnight and disappeared into the darkness of his room. He recollected seeing a small naval telescope in the loft when he explored there. Tomorrow he would return to the loft and bring the telescope down to the bedroom, more to get a better look at the guy than anything else.

At seven-thirty the following evening Bill stationed himself on his chair in the darkness to await the appearance of the woman. As he had hoped, she came into view. Bill stood and made his presence known by waving to her. She acknowledged him with a wave back.

Holding the telescope up to his face in mock presentation, as if he was looking through it, he then lowered it and pointed to the woman, holding the palms of his hands upwards in an enquiring manner. He hoped that his version of the international language would be understood without offence being taken.

The woman held her finger to her chin for a second and then smiled in recognition of his message. She pointed to Bill, then held a pretend telescope up to her eye, then pointed to herself. Bill held one thumb in the air and the woman immediately reciprocated with a two thumb consent.

She waited while Bill extended the telescope to its full length and then, laughing, assumed several different poses while he watched and laughed with her.

A friendship had been made.

Each night, before going to bed, the two met and waved and she posed and laughed. Then one night the woman reached under her mattress and extracted a sheet of paper. Holding this up in front of her Bill read the words she had written.

'Meet me down at the bridge tomorrow?'

Taken by surprise Bill thought for a second then pointed to his watch and held his palms up in enquiry. The woman quickly scribbled something on the sheet of paper and held it up, once more.

'2:30?'

Bill gave the now familiar two thumb acknowledgement.

At two-twenty the following day Bill made his way down to the bridge over the trout stream. The woman was already there, sat on the bankside. She stood and smiled a broad smile with perfect white teeth as he approached.

He went to give her a hug, but she stepped back and said, "No. We shouldn't. I'm married."

His face took on a puzzled look and she responded with, "He has many faults, but I can't cheat on him."

Bill gave a shrug of approval and they both sat on the bank side.

"What's your name?" he asked. "Mine's Bill."

She smiled and turned to him. "You look like a Bill, but I don't mind if you don't…" she said with a cheeky look on her face. Despite her previous comment, Bill was sure she was flirting with him.

"My name is Charlotte."

"Hello, Charlotte. I'm pleased to meet you. Tell me all about yourself."

The two sat on the bank side for a couple of hours, chatting and getting to know each other. They swapped stories of their families and working life, although Charlotte didn't have much of a working life because her husband forbade her from leaving the cottage. He was out, presently, and would not be returning 'till late. She didn't know where he went during the day, but she enjoyed what little freedom she had while he was out.

"Why don't you leave him?" enquired Bill.

"I can't. He'll find me," she answered, with a resigned sigh.

Bill didn't feel there was any need to make Charlotte unhappy, so he quickly changed the subject and the two chatted happily.

Bill mentioned that he hadn't yet seen any of the other neighbours, despite having been resident in the manor for several weeks. Charlotte gossiped about the goings on in the little hamlet.

"You should keep an eye on Alaska Rose Cottage. You'll be surprised at what you see," she joked.

The two continued their chats and laughter and light-hearted banter.

After a while she suddenly sat up with a worried look on her face.

"He's coming back!" she exclaimed and jumped to her feet. "I've got to go. If he finds me out here there'll be hell to pay," she said. "Keep your telescope on my window. I may not be there for a while, but I will show myself again, I promise."

With that she hurried up the bank and dashed towards her cottage.

Bill sat there for some time, pondering over Charlotte's wretched fear of the man she shared her cottage with. He disliked that man immensely and given the chance he would show him just how much he disliked him.

That chance wasn't long in coming. He heard the scraping of hob-nailed boots on the road approaching the bridge. Not wishing to show his hand too soon, Bill hid under the bridge until the noise of the bloke's boots passed over him and up towards the cottages.

On his way over the bridge the bully growled in a gravelly, menacing voice, "I know you're hiding under there!"

How much Bill would have liked to confront this bully was shown in his tightly balled fists, but now wasn't the time.

The bully would get his just deserts and be punished in due course. Bill was sure of that.

Bill estimated Charlotte's age to be in her mid-to-late 20s. He and Charlotte met most nights via the telescope. They posed stupid poses, pulled faces and generally laughed at each other's antics.

They also met down at the bridge on the occasions when the bully was away from home. They talked about nothing in particular, just passing the time of the day and enjoying each other's company, although she would never get close enough for Bill to give her a friendly hug. He wasn't too phased out by this. Many people didn't like such familiarity. The way she looked down when Bill held his arms wide for a hug, however, made him think that she really did want to be held close, but she always reminded him that the bully was in the background of her mind.

One day he offered her his arms, as he usually did when they met in person. She again declined the hug, but she looked up from her usual frown, smiled a happy smile and said to him, enthusiastically, "Tell you what... Meet me through the telescope tonight."

Bill was somewhat puzzled by this. They usually did meet via the telescope, even if she was unable to get to the bridge.

That night Bill made himself comfortable in his 'viewing' chair and waited until Charlotte came into view, puzzled by her comment.

She usually wore her day clothes when they met, whether via the telescope or down at the bridge. Tonight, she entered her bedroom in a dressing gown tied at the waist, her long blonde hair cascading onto her shoulders. Waving to Bill, she blew a Marilyn Munroe kiss to him and stood there for a moment, laughing.

At first Bill didn't know what she was going to do… Until she slowly pulled the dressing gown cord undone and dropped it to the floor. Bill could see her flimsy full-length nightdress peeking out from her dressing gown. She was staring at the floor, and she slowly looked up, smiled her appealing smile and pulled a sheet of paper from the dressing gown pocket. On it was written just one word;

'MORE?'

Laughing, Bill gave her the thumbs up.

She reciprocated by slowly opening the dressing gown, unhooked it from her shoulders and dropped it to the floor. She stood there in a statuesque pose as Bill rose to his feet and gave her a standing ovation, thinking that must be the end of the performance.

Not so. She bent forward to retrieve the note from the windowsill, once more holding it up for Bill to read.

'MORE?'

Bill drew a sharp breath. He really wasn't expecting this. Standing in front of his window, mouth open, he was rooted to the spot.

Charlotte didn't wait for his reply, she slowly started to undo the buttons of her night dress. Working from the top down she undid a button, opened a bit of the night dress and teased Bill by licking her lips or blowing a kiss before progressing on to the next button. Bill was mesmerised. Unable to move. He watched in eager anticipation as she slowly unbuttoned her night dress until she reached down to undo the last button. She straightened up and allowed Bill to soak up the scene she had created, the night gown tantalisingly open to reveal just a hint of her exquisite figure.

The moon had climbed over the roof of the manor, and it had now illuminated Charlotte's bedroom to the extent that Bill didn't even need to use the telescope. Seeing her, standing there and smiling at him, he was overwhelmed by her desire to make him happy.

She bent forward again to retrieve the note and held it up for him to read.

'MORE?'

Bill was speechless. Rooted to the spot. Paralysed.

She didn't wait for an answer. She slowly and evocatively peeled the nightdress back and dropped it to the floor, exposing every inch of her naked body to Bill.

He was mesmerised by her moonlit beauty. She opened her arms to display her perfectly formed breasts and shapely body, enhanced by her long, golden tresses and wide, paper white smile. Like an overhead stage light, the moon bathed her in its brightness as she allowed Bill to soak up her beauty. It seemed, from where Bill stood, that her whole body glowed… A ghostly, angelic glow that took his breath away.

The only thing that marred this angelic vision of beauty was the purple bruise on her right side where she had been kicked. She tried to hide this by covering it with her hand, but she was unsuccessful.

After what seemed to be forever, she waved a goodbye to Bill and slowly retreated backwards, her dressing gown having been picked up and draped over her arm. Melding into the darkness of the adjoining landing, Bill lost sight of her. He collapsed into his viewing chair, feeling exhausted by the show that Charlotte had just put on for his benefit.

Sitting there, reflecting on the night's activity he heard the familiar sound of hob nailed boots scraping on the gravel courtyard. Bully had returned for his nightly fix of abasement. Whenever he returned from his time away from the cottage, he humiliated Charlotte by shouting at her and making her perform sexual acts on him.

It didn't take long for him to appear in the bedroom, followed by Charlotte in her dressing gown. He saw the nightdress on the floor, picked it up and threw it at her. As he stormed out of the room, she quickly put the nightdress back into a drawer. Bully returned with a towel wrapped around his fist and pushed her back against the bedroom wall. He roughly slapped her face with his free hand then beat her, mercilessly, with the towel wrapped fist.

Picking her up from where she had fallen, he stripped the dressing gown from her body and threw her on the bed, forcing himself upon her. Roughly forcing his erection into her Bill saw the pain on her face. After a while he roughly turned her over and entered her from behind. When he got tired of this, he slapped her face several times and forced her mouth over his erection, holding her hair to stop her pulling away.

Bill, stunned and angrily gritting his teeth, silently watched this abuse until it stopped. There had to be a way of saving Charlotte from the abuse of this maniac, but he didn't know how. Tomorrow he would contact Wally to see if he had any suggestions.

The bully got off the bed and pulled his trousers back on. He spat on Charlotte as he left the room.

Charlotte painfully eased herself off the bed and put her dressing gown back on. She turned to face the window and looked out of it towards Bill. He clenched his fists and shook with anger as he saw how she had changed. She was broken, a mess, her face bloodied, and her body covered in welts and bruises where she had been beaten. Her hair was dishevelled, her lips were swollen and split from the constant punches, and he could see tears running down her cheeks. She wiped the blood from the corner of her mouth with the back of her hand. The only thing that looked new and clean and fresh was the gold Saint Christopher medallion hanging from her bruised neck, glistening in the moonlight.

The angel he had seen, not thirty minutes earlier, was no more.

Chapter 15

The following morning Bill decided to walk into town to have breakfast at the tea house.

Mel smiled her usual greeting as Bill sat at his usual table. Without asking, she went into the kitchen and returned a few minutes later with a full English breakfast. She sat with Bill and talked about mundane things until he had emptied his plate, wiped his bread round the plate's rim to soak up the remnants of the fried egg and sat back with a contented smile. Taking the plate back to the kitchen she returned with a steaming pot of tea and two cups.

"What have you been up to?" she asked.

"Not a lot," answered Bill, "just cleaning up the manor."

"You're not sleeping in that old wreck, are you?" she asked in amazement.

"Why not? I've cleaned up a few rooms and it's not too bad."

"You're a braver person than me," she laughed.

"I've slept in worse. When I was in the army, I spent six months in a tent. At least I have some running water up at the manor."

"Well, you know you can always crash here, if needs be."

Their friendship had developed into something good in the time that Bill had known Mel. They had bonded easily and looked forward to chatting across the cafe table whenever Bill visited. Neither of them pre-judged the other or intruded into their private lives by asking awkward questions. They were now at ease with each other and thoroughly enjoyed each other's company.

"What do you know about the manor?" he asked.

"Not much. I told you. It's been like that since before I was a kid. But local gossip has it that that field has got quite a history. I'm sure there's something written about it somewhere, but I've not bothered to look. Our parents always told us not to go anywhere near it."

"But I thought you went on to the field?"

"Only as far as the bridge. That corner of the field is nice and private, you know. We'll have to go there together, some time, and you'll see just how private it is…" She put a hand on his thigh.

That cinched it. Bill now knew that she wasn't just flirting. Their friendship, it seemed, may well have progressed to the next level.

"Whoa!" he smiled, looking down at Mel's hand. "We've only just got to know each other," he joked. Was he being defensive?

Chuckling, she replied, "So? I like older men…" She then winced a painful face and corrected herself. "What I meant was, I like you."

Bill grinned and retorted, "Yeah. That's what they all say."

Mel gave his arm a gentle slap as a reprimand for kidding her.

Bill returned to their conversation. "Tell me about your family."

"Not much to tell, really. I was born here, in Colbert Village, in 1985. In this place…," waving her arm around the room.

"It was just a cottage back then. When mum died, she left it to me and I had it converted to what you see now. Downstairs there's this room and a kitchen. Upstairs there are two bedrooms, one with an en suite shower. Want to see it?" she teased.

"No…" answered Bill with raised eyebrows and a smile.

"The other room is my spare bedroom," continued Mel.

"Any siblings?"

"I once had an older sister, but she died when she was in her late twenties. She hung herself from a roof beam in her bedroom."

"I'm sorry. Do you want to talk about it?"

"Oh, there's nothing to tell. They said she had committed suicide as a result of a partnership gone wrong, but no-one really knows what happened. She was clutching something in her hand, but the police wouldn't say what."

Bill looked at Mel's downturned face and decided to change the subject.

"Got any of those blueberry muffins?"

"For you, yes." The smile had returned to her face.

"Has this place got a police station," asked Bill.

"Why, are you going to turn yourself in?" laughed Mel.

"Yeah. Didn't I tell you? I'm a serial clothesline thief. I've got quite a collection of women's underwear," he joked.

"Stop it!" she reprimanded and went to fetch a couple of muffins and a refill of tea from the kitchen.

When she sat down at the table, once more, Bill again asked, "Well? Is there a police station anywhere here?"

Mel described the route to the station. It was tucked away, behind the cottages and shops lining the main street. Bill was pleased to be told that it was usually manned in the daytime but closed at night. The resident policeman was a Sergeant Manning.

After paying for his breakfast Bill walked through the village, turned off the main street and approached the little country police station.

On his way there he felt slightly uncomfortable as he observed the residents of Colbert Village staring at him as they passed by. He was waylaid by an elderly couple who asked if he was the gentleman who had inherited the field.

"Yes," answered Bill, thinking, *'I bet there aren't any secrets in this place.'*

"Mel told us about you," the woman said." She's a lovely girl, isn't she?"

"Err, yes, I guess so," answered Bill, with just a hint of embarrassment.

After passing a few minutes of the day chatting amiably, the couple smiled their farewells and Bill continued his journey to the police station, thinking what a nice couple they were.

Inside he was met by an imposing police sergeant who looked up from his paperwork, surprised by an unexpected visitor, and asked, "Can I help you, sir?"

Bill drew in a breath and paused briefly while he thought of how to approach the subject he was here to discuss.

"My name's Bill Colbert. How do I report an assault?"

"You've come to the right place, sir. Can we start by taking down a few details?" the sergeant asked as he wrote down Bill's name on the top sheet of a lined pad, conveniently placed on his desk in front of him.

"You're the gentleman that has recently inherited Colbert's Field, aren't you?"

Bill wondered where the hell these people were getting this information.

"Yes, that's right."

"And what's your address?"

"I'm currently staying at Colbert's Manor."

"Oh? At the manor, you say? I bet that's nice and comfortable for you?" asked the sergeant with a hint of sarcasm and a look of puzzlement on his face. He made notes on his pad that were unreadable from Bill's angle.

"It's okay. It'll be a lot better when it's been properly cleaned up."

"If you say so, sir. Now then, what is it you want to tell me about a person being assaulted?"

"Her name is Charlotte…"

The sergeant looked up in surprise and interrupted Bill's flow of words.

"Would that be *the* Charlotte…Charlotte from Iceberg Rose Cottage?" queried the Sergeant.

"That's her. She was the person being abused. She is both mentally and physically abused most days by some bloke. I've witnessed it on several occasions."

"I see, sir. I think you must be mistaken."

This comment didn't sit right with Bill. He studied the sergeant for a few seconds then asked, "Are you going to do anything about it?"

"Are you presently taking any medication, sir?"

This last question, and its insinuation, infuriated Bill.

"What? What's that got to do with anything. No, I'm not taking any medication. I'm not a druggy, or an alcoholic, or a dementia patient, or schizophrenic. I'm perfectly sane. I've not escaped from a mental institution, and I've come here to genuinely report an assault," he shouted.

"No need to shout, sir," the sergeant responded calmly.

After a pause to allow Bill to calm down he asked, "… And where did this assault take place?" writing notes and taking a deep breath that was slowly exhaled through puffed out cheeks.

"I saw it through the bedroom window of her cottage," Bill replied.

The sergeant stopped writing, dropped his pen onto the pad and looked at Bill with narrowed eyes. Bill realised the implication of his last statement.

Shaking his head he submitted, "It's not what you think. I was cleaning my windows yesterday and …"

The sergeant held up his hand to stop Bill mid-sentence. In the ensuing silence he returned to his lined pad to make more unreadable notes. After a couple of minutes, he looked up and stared into Bill's face with a furrowed brow.

"Well?" asked Bill.

Folding his arms, the policeman nodded his head two or three times, breathed out another long, cheek puffed-out sigh and then answered Bill.

"Leave it with me, Mr. Colbert. I'll look into it."

After another long pause the two men eyed each other suspiciously. The sergeant didn't instil any confidence in Bill with his condescending response.

Bill decided that he was not going to get any further with this exchange and he turned and left the police station.

Chapter 16

February 2023.

The office refurbishment was now in full swing but the flat still wasn't ready to occupy. Bill continued to commute between Colbert Village and the office occasionally to drop off and pick up work to do at the manor. Elle had tired of asking Bill if she could visit, so she stopped. She was sure Bill would invite her in his own time.

Bill had been to see Wally about the events he had witnessed and his conversation with Sergeant Manning. Wally was clearly too busy to dedicate any time to the events, but he did, nonetheless, listen to what Bill had to say.

"I'm sure he'll look into it," Wally offered.

"But he didn't believe a word I said," complained Bill. "He treated me in a most condescending manner, as if I was off my trolley. He even intimated that I was a druggy!"

"I'm sure he didn't mean that. It sounds as if he was just making the routine type of enquiries that I make. People can be pretty fractious at times."

"Okay, I take that on board, but do you think he will update me on progress?"

"Doubtful. He might follow up some time, even if it's just to go round there and speak to the lady off the record, but the chances of anything being done to the guy are remote."

"Surely, that kind of abuse is illegal. It's an assault. Bodily injury and all that."

"Yes, it is. Today, almost any kind of abuse is illegal, but you must bear in mind that we don't like to get involved in domestic fracas. Unless the woman, herself, makes a formal complaint in person there is nothing that the sergeant can do to help her. He might have a quiet word in the guy's shell-like, but that approach doesn't usually work. The guy will calm down for about two minutes then he'll be back to his old self again."

"It seems so unfair. From what you say, she's got to be killed by this guy before anyone will do anything to put him away."

"That's about it, I'm afraid."

The two parted company with Bill feeling dissatisfied by what Wally had told him, not that Wally could do anything himself because the offence didn't take place on his turf.

Bill just had to hope that he can persuade Charlotte to either make a formal complaint against the guy or leave him.

After looking in on Elle he returned to the manor.

Chapter 17

Pilgrim Rose Cottage

The following morning Bill went for his usual post breakfast walk to take in the crisp February air and get his thoughts in order for work.

As he passed Pilgrim Rose Cottage, he saw a young boy sat on its front doorstep. Sat there, without a topcoat, he shivered in the cold air. He looked about seven to eight years old, and his shivering wasn't a surprise to Bill because he was dressed only in short trousers and a shirt under a hand knitted pullover. He had no shoes or socks on. He was absentmindedly digging a small hole in the soil with a bone-handled hunting knife.

"Are you okay?" asked Bill, a concerned look on his face.

The boy looked up and nodded.

"Do your parents know you're out here without your shoes and socks?"

Once more, the boy just nodded.

"Is your mum at home?" enquired Bill.

At last, the boy spoke. "Dad's made me sit here until he's finished breakfast."

"What? Why?"

"I spilt some milk."

Bill could not believe what he had just been told.

"Does your mom know?"

"Yes."

"Can you tell me your name?"

"Ezra," answered the boy.

Bill moved forward to rap on the cottage door. Before he got close the door opened and a mean looking guy poked his head through the gap.

"You can come inside now," he growled at the boy without looking up at Bill.

Ezra stood and went back into the cottage, head bowed.

The guy looked Bill up and down menacingly. As Bill moved forward to speak to him, the guy slammed the door closed before Bill could utter a word.

As Bill turned to leave, he heard the boy yelp in pain behind the closed cottage door.

One evening, during a telescope meeting with Charlotte, Bill saw some movement in the downstairs window of Pilgrim Rose Cottage. With the telescope he could see more of the internal rooms of the cottages, not that he nosed in on any cottage other than Charlotte's. But Bill's interest in Pilgrim Rose Cottage was piqued when he had met Ezra… And his dad.

Homing in on the downstairs window he noticed how the occupants appeared to be living in a 1970s-time bubble. Everything in the front room; its wallpaper, its furniture, its carpets and even the clothes that the people wore all reflected the style of the 70s. The floral patterns of this bygone age jumped out at Bill and shouted 'Retro!'

Bill watched with interest as Ezra and his mother sat in front of the open fire, she busily knitting something, and he is playing on the hearth rug with some little plastic soldiers. He looked to be about six or seven years old, but although his mum was probably in her early 30s, she looked a lot older. The years had not been kind to her.

The dad entered the room and shoved Ezra out of the way with his foot as he made his way to the chair opposite mum. Ezra regained his kneeling position, collected his soldiers up and crawled under the table. There, he continued his pretend war game, looking up at his parents occasionally to make sure they were not heading in his direction.

Bill couldn't help thinking that not even a dog deserved such treatment. In fact, the interaction between the man and the boy mirrored exactly how a dog would behave. Mum just sat there in silence and Bill wondered if she would speak up for the boy. No chance. She just continued to knit and talked to her husband as if Ezra didn't exist.

Thinking back to the time Elle was Ezra's age, he wondered how anyone can treat a child that way.

As Ezra continued his game, he surreptitiously made his way towards the warm fireplace. Mum had gone to the kitchen to fetch a mug of tea for her husband. The guy sat this on his knee and steadied it with one hand while he munched biscuits with the other.

The boy's game increased in intensity; his hands thrown outwards as each pretend explosion happened. Lost in this pretend world he exploded another bomb, this time a massive bomb, and as his hands parted to emulate the effects of the explosion, he accidentally nudged his dad's knee, spilling some tea onto his trousers.

Dad jumped up while still holding his mug, spilling its contents onto the carpet in front of the boy. The boy immediately scrambled back under the table, quickly followed by the mug that punched the middle of his back.

Dad dragged Ezra out from under the table and vented his anger on the boy by beating him mercilessly. His anger vented, the man roughly shoved Eza towards the doorway with his boot's toecap. Ezra picked himself up and hurriedly scampered upstairs to get away from the man's foot.

Bill followed him upstairs with the telescope. He saw him reappear in the front bedroom. As if the beating downstairs wasn't enough, mum entered the bedroom with a cane and proceeded to whip Ezra's upturned bottom as he lay face down on the bed. The boy screamed in agony with each lash of the cane.

Bill felt sick. He shook with anger and vowed to contact social services the following day with a view to having the boy removed. If necessary, he would instruct solicitors to make sure that Ezra was placed into safe care, away from his obnoxious and violent parents.

It was now eleven p.m. Bill decided to bed down for the night.

He doubted that he would sleep much, after what he had just witnessed, but at least Pilgrim Rose Cottage was quiet… For the time being.

At five-thirty the following morning Bill got up to go to the toilet. Returning to the bedroom he noticed the bedroom light was on in Pilgrim Rose Cottage. Interested, he sat in his 'viewing' chair, telescope at the ready.

Looking at the book nestling between the parents it appeared that one of them had fallen asleep while reading, leaving the bedroom light on in the process.

What followed was Bill's worse nightmare as he watched Ezra enter his parents' bedroom with an axe and smash it into his dad's skull. The bed shook violently as dad convulsed in his death throes, his blood and brains oozing onto his pillow.

The shaking mattress woke mum. She turned over to see what going on and screamed her husband's name as she saw the mess on his pillow, the blood and gore now freely flowing from the large incision in his skull onto the mattress under his shoulder. The shock of what she was looking at blotted out Ezra's form as he dropped the axe and walked out of the room.

Bill followed him into the corridor and down the stairs. Ezra disappeared into the kitchen.

Focusing the telescope back on the bedroom he searched for mum. She was nowhere to be seen. After what seemed to be an eternity, a downstairs light lit up the room and Bill saw Mum pick up the telephone handset. She dialled a number which Bill took to be 999 and after hysterically shouting at the handset she dropped it and stood there in utter shock, her head in her hands.

Ezra entered the room, his hand behind his back.

"What have you done?" cried mum.

Ezra just stood there, looking up at his hysterical mum.

"Why did you do it, you little wretch," she demanded.

Still no response from Ezra.

Mum grabbed his shoulders roughly and shouted curses into his impassive face. "You evil little bastard!" she hissed, in between face slaps. "What's wrong with you?"

Releasing his shoulders from her grip she bunched the front of his pyjama jacket in her hands and ejected her malevolence into his face through globules of spit. "I should have drowned you the moment you were born," she spat at him, teeth clenched in anger. "You're nothing but a waste of space, you good-for-nothing little shit. We never wanted you in the first place."

The anger in her wide-open eyes burned into Ezra's emotionless face.

Tears ran down his cheek as he lifted his arm and thrust the bone-handled hunting knife into his mum's throat.

In utter shock, Bill sat in his chair, undecided about what he should do. As he stood to go down to the cottage, he heard the distant sound of police sirens.

He sat in his chair for the rest of the night and watched many police cars arrive at the cottage. Bill couldn't help thinking that the vehicles he saw arriving at the cottage were also trapped in a time bubble. Each one, including the two ambulances, all looking like retro models of the vehicles that were prevalent in the 70s.

He watched as Ezra was taken away in a police car.

Chapter 18

Bill didn't see the need to report Ezra's abuse. The police would find out soon enough when they start to interview him, although Bill doubted that Ezra would be in any fit state to be interviewed for some time, given his condition when the police arrive. When he was being put into the back seat of the police car Bill couldn't help noticing the blank stare in the child's eyes. Absolutely nothing behind, or in front, of them. Just a wide-eyed stare into oblivion. Ezra was clearly in a dark place. Bill couldn't help feeling sorry for him, wondering what his future might hold for him.

Bill's thoughts, however, were brought back to the present when he realised that he was a witness to the murders. On second thoughts, perhaps he should re-visit the police station. It would give him an opportunity to get an update on Charlotte's abuse case.

The following morning, he went into the village to get his now daily breakfast from the tearoom.

Enjoying his breakfast chat with Mel, her demeanour suddenly changed when he mentioned Charlotte's name. She sat opposite Bill in a quiet mode, not speaking unless it was absolutely necessary. After a while, Bill noticed the change in Mel's emotions. She sat, head bowed, looking down at her interlaced fingers resting on her lap.

"Are you okay? You've gone all quiet on me," asked Bill.

"Yes, just thinking."

Bill tried to lighten the conversation.

"O' oh. Danger! Thinking woman just entered the room!"

Mel looked up with tears on her cheeks, stood up and disappeared into the kitchen.

Bill immediately became anxious. This was not like Mel. She was always happy, smiling, exchanging amusing insults with him. Thinking he might have said something to offend her, he got up from his seat and followed her into the kitchen to find her propped against a counter, wiping the tears away.

"I'm sorry. I didn't mean to upset you. I was only joking."

"I know you were. It's not your fault, Bill. I just felt a bit sad, that's all."

"Oh? Sad about what?"

"Nothing. I'll get over it. I'll tell you some other time."

"It doesn't look like 'nothing', Mel. Is there anything I can do to make you feel better?"

"Yes, there is."

"Tell me. Just tell me what to do."

"Kiss me…"

As soon as Bill entered the police station Sergeant Manning looked up from his desk and gave him a patronizing smile. A smile that said 'Not him, again.'

"Good morning, Mr. Colbert. What can I do for you today?"

"I've come to give a witness statement about Ezra's murder of his parents."

Manning looked down at his desktop. A long stare that said 'Is this guy for real?' With narrow eyes and a suspicious gaze on his face, Manning looked back up at Bill's face and replied, "Oh, really. Would you mind stepping into the interview room, sir?"

Bill followed the policeman into the interview room and sat at the empty desk. Manning had brought a writing pad with him and sat opposite Bill, pen at the ready.

"Okay, Mr. Colbert, in your own time ..."

Bill spoke no more than a few sentences when Manning held up his hand. Bill stopped speaking and waited for Manning to speak.

"Tell you what, sir. Why don't you write down what you want to say while I go to make us a cup of tea?" pushing the pad and pen across the table to Bill.

Bill started to write as Manning left the room.

The policeman re-entered the room after about fifteen minutes, holding a tray with a teapot and a couple of mugs on top. Bill held out his statement for the sergeant to take, but Manning ignored it.

"Shall I pour?" asked Manning.

"Yes, thank you," still holding up the ignored statement.

Manning sat down and poured the tea. Bill patiently waited for Manning to take the statement. There was clearly a stalemate here that nobody wanted to break.

After a few sips of tea, while Manning silently interrogated Bill's face, he took the statement from Bill and sat there reading it, looking nonchalant. Bill sat quietly, ignoring his mug of tea.

After reading Bill's statement Manning stood up and left the room, once more, without looking at Bill. He took Bill's statement with him. Bill sat with his arms folded across his chest until Manning returned with a file, about ten minutes later, and took up his position across from Bill. Opening the file, he read a few of the documents inside it and then looked up at Bill.

"You saw all this last night, you say." This was more of an announcement than a question.

"Yes."

"May I ask, sir, are you still sleeping in the manor?"

"Yes. Why, is that a problem for you?"

"No, sir. Absolutely not. I would have thought it was more of a problem for you."

"No, not really. Are you happy with my statement?"

"I'm happy if you're happy, Mr. Colbert."

Bill now felt distinctly uncomfortable with the way Manning was treating him. Manning's off-handed approach to the questions and answers put to Bill were, to Bill's mind, confirmation that Manning disbelieved what he had written in his statement.

Bill took the bull by the horns and challenged Manning.

"Look, Sergeant. I'm just trying to be a good citizen here, but you're not making it easy with your condescending manner and inane questions. What have I done to upset you?"

"Nothing, sir. I'm sorry if you think that."

"Is there anything wrong with my statement? I'm quite happy to change it if you think I should."

"No, sir. No need for that. It's quite a comprehensive and detailed statement of events."

Bill decided that he was going to get nowhere with this chap. "Can I go now?" he asked.

"Of course, sir. You're not under arrest."

Manning put Bill's statement in the file and closed the cover. He gave Bill another of his patronising smiles.

Bill stood to leave the room. He stopped as he approached the door and asked, "What's happening about the assault I reported?"

"Oh, we're still looking into that. We'll let you know in due course, sir."

Bill left the police station dejectedly, thinking *'What the hell is the matter with that man?'*

He decided to go see Wally, once more, to get his opinion of today's meeting with Manning.

On the train to London Bill got a call from Julie, his secretary.

"Hello, Bill. I thought you would like to know that the Coroner's report has just been delivered here."

That's great, Julie. Can you hang on to it until I arrive? I'm on the train to London right now."

"Will do. Do you want Elle to see it?"

"No, not yet. I'll look at it as soon as I land."

It's now six months since the fire and Bill had wondered what he could do to speed things up. It seemed that the Coroner had decided to get off his chair and finish the report.

Elle was talking to Julie when Bill exited the lift, and she greeted him with a hug and a peck on the cheek. He was greeted with more hugs and handshakes when he walked into the main office. He had extracted the Coroner's report from Julie on his way past.

"Is that the Coroner's report?" Elle asked.

She already knew that it was because Julie had mentioned its arrival, although Julie had declined to hand it over to Elle, in accordance with Bills wishes.

"Yes, it is. Give me a few minutes to get settled and read it, then come round to my room to talk about it."

"Okay. How did they know to deliver it here and not to the house?"

"'Cos I told 'em to."

"Oh. Okay. See you later." Elle went to her office.

Bill sat at his desk and Brad entered the room.

"Hi, Bill. How's things?"

"Not bad. How's work?" Anything I need to do while I'm here?"

"There's a backlog of reports to check. Bill, I'm sorry to dump this stuff on you. I know you should be doing better things, but you did say that you'd tell me when you are ready to get back in the saddle. Are you ready yet?"

"No, not at the moment. I've got other things happening that need my attention. I don't mind the report checking, honestly. If it enables the workers to get on with making a profit then I'll keep going, for the time being. Just let me know if you think I should do something more constructive."

"Will do. Is that the Coroner's report?"

"Yeah. Give me about ten minutes to read it then come back in here with Elle."

"Okay."

Brad left Bill to read the Coroner's report. As he was reading, Julie came into the room with a stack of files, on top of which were a stack of telephone messages. She put them all on the corner of the desk without disturbing Bill from his reading.

When he finished reading the report he sat back and thought to himself, "That's not going to go down well."

He picked up the telephone messages and skimmed through them. Putting them into appropriate piles of related workmates he dumped the rubbish into the waste bin and kept two for himself. One was from Wally which he put to one side. He will be meeting Wally this afternoon. He called Julie into his room.

"Julie, I've got a message here from a Hugo MacEnrie. Do you know who this guy is, or what he wants?"

"He just asked if you were in and left his number. Isn't he the guy at Amy's workplace? The one you saw last September?"

"Oh, yea. I'd forgotten about him. I'll call in on him this afternoon."

Elle and Brad sat in the easy chairs in Bill's office waiting for Bill to make the first move. Bill paused while he thought of what to tell them.

"Just read the Coroner's report on Amy's death," he said. After another short pause he decided to come right out with it. "She didn't die from smoke inhalation or from being burnt. She was suffocated before the fire was started."

Both exclaiming, "What…?" in unison. Elle and Brad shot different questions to Bill, all at the same time.

How? Who? Why? When? At home? What with? Did she know the person? Did she suffer? Did she struggle?

Bill held his hand up to silence them.

"I doubt the Coroner can answer any of those questions. I certainly can't, but I'm meeting Wally this afternoon and I'll take a copy of the report with me."

Elle spoke up. "Dad, we have to find out who did this, and why."

Bill nodded.

"I intend to…" he responded.

Chapter 19

On his way to Wally's office, he called into Globe Publications.

Approaching the receptionist he asked, "Can you ask Hugo MacEnrie if he's got a few minutes to see me?"

"Yes, sir. Please, take a seat and I'll let him know you're here."

Bill sat in one of the reception chairs, patiently reading the newspaper. After maybe fifteen minutes he looked up from his paper and saw Hugo stood halfway down the stairs to first floor level, looking at him.

Bill had no idea how long Hugo had been standing there because he hadn't indicated his arrival. Slightly unnerved, Bill folded the newspaper and placed it on the low-level table next to him. Standing, he made his way towards the staircase. Hugo continued his journey to meet him, hand outstretched and a smile on his face in a welcome gesture.

Hugo invited Bill to sit at the table, once more.

"It's nice to meet you again, Bill. How can I help?"

Bill didn't exactly believe Hugo was as sincere as he made out to be.

"I've got a message to contact you," waving the post-It note to Hugo. "I'm sorry I haven't responded before now, but I've been away from the office for a while."

"That's okay. I was just following up on the fire at your place. Do they know any more yet?"

Bill assumed that '… *they*' referred to the police or Fire Brigade.

"No, not yet" Bill lied. He didn't want anyone other than essential persons to know about the Fire Brigade and Coroner's reports.

"Oh, well," replied Hugo, "I was just interested, that's all."

Bill noted that Hugo's roots needed touching up with some more Grecian 2000.

It occurred to Bill that this meeting may be an opportunity to follow up on Elle's allegation of Amy's infidelity... *'Might be worth a punt,'* he thought to himself.

With a straight-laced face, Bill asked, "Do you know if Amy was having an affair with someone in the office?"

"No … God no! What makes you think that?"

"Oh, it's just a rumour," replied Bill. He sat there waiting for Hugo to speak. It wasn't long.

"…There is a rumour around this place that David and Amy were spending a lot of time together."

"Oh? …"

"Yeah. You know that they often went away on 'business' trips?" dipping his fingers in the air euphemistically referring to 'business'.

"Do you think there's any smoke with that, or is it just gossip?"

"I… I… I don't know. Do you want me to ask around for you?"

"No, it's okay. It was just a thought, that's all."

Goodbyes were made and Bill left the office. Crossing over the road he paused on the other side, turned and looked at Globe's office building, deep in thought. He was sure he saw David March duck behind the window reveal to his office.

Was there any smoke in what Hugo had just told him, or was it just office chit chat? Bill put it on the back burners for now and made a mental note to follow it up some time.

Sat opposite Wally, Bill waited patiently while Wally called for Amy's file and signed a few reports.

When the file arrived Wally opened it, studied a few pages then turned to Bill.

"Okay. We've received a copy of the Coroner's report," confirmed Wally.

Bill asked, "Have you read it yet?"

"Nope. Only just got the file back from forensics. Can you give me a couple of minutes?"

"Sure."

Wally asked his secretary for a couple of coffees and sat back to digest the Coroner's report first, then the forensic report.

When he finished, he looked stern-faced at Bill and puffed a large breath through his cheeks.

"What do forensics say?" asked Bill.

"This has become an active investigation, so I can't tell you anything, Bill."

"Hang on, Wally. This is me you're talking to, not some newspaper reporter that's going to splash my life over the front page. What does the forensic report say?" anger beginning to rise in Bill's voice.

Wally put his elbow on the desk and supported his brow with his left hand.

"What does the Coroner's report tell you, Bill?"

"That Amy's death was no accident."

"Correct. Have you read it all?"

"Of course, I have. What are you getting at, Wally?"

"If you've read it all you will have seen that there was trace evidence of ether in her lungs."

"Yes, I got that.?"

"You'll also have read that she was suffocated before the fire started."

Bill stared in silence as he mulled over Wally's comments.

"Okay, got that, as well," responded Bill in a lowered voice.

Wally sat looking at Bill, trying to think of what to say next.

"We also found trace elements of acetate on the remnants of the bedclothes."

Bill looked at Wally without speaking.

"You know that acetate is highly flammable?"

"Yeah?…"

Wally sat back to let Bill absorb the information.

Bill gave it a couple of seconds, then proffered, "… So you think acetate was used to start the fire?"

Wally put down his pen and leaned forward.

"I didn't tell you that, Bill, and if it comes out anywhere, I'll deny all knowledge of this conversation, okay?" Wally warned.

"Okay. You have my word. I'll not tell a soul."

"You cannot even tell Elle. At least not 'til we've completed our investigations. It's now a murder enquiry…

"We think that Amy was put under with ether and suffocated with a pillow before acetate was splashed over her. The Coroner's report say that she was probably dead when the explosion occurred, but that's not all."

"What else have you got?"

"A search of the wreckage confirms that the gas taps had been left on. Not just one tap, all of them, but we found something else that doesn't make much sense."

Bill sat there dumbfounded. "What?" he asked.

"A detailed examination of the entry door and surrounding frame confirms that there was no damage to either of these elements. This can only mean that Amy let the perp' into the house voluntarily."

Flashes of what Elle and Hugo had told him painted a picture in Bill's mind of Amy opening the door and smiling to someone, but who?

Wally continued, "Putting it all together, it seems that whoever Amy let into the house had put her to sleep on the bed with the ether, suffocated her, splashed a lot of acetate over her… Probably in the region of a pint, then lit it and went downstairs to turn on the kitchen gas taps. Given time, the whole house would have filled with gas if all the windows were closed.

"The fire that was started in the bedroom will most likely have been the one that ignited the gas. The resulting explosion demolished the house and the fire continued to burn until the Fire Brigade arrived. The neighbours put a call out to them and us at six forty-five."

By way of a mollifying statement Wally looked at Bill and said, "It's probable that Amy never felt a thing."

"Acetate? isn't that used in the publishing industry?" enquired Bill.

"Maybe. We'd have to check. Why?"

"There's a strong rumour that she may have been having an affair with somebody at work."

"Where'd you get that?

"Elle told me about the affair, but some guy in her office is pushing me towards the MD."

"It's a start. An affair is always a good start, but I, personally, wouldn't have put any credence in that rumour, knowing Amy. I'll get somebody to do a few searches on the employees. I'll need to get a court order first, though."

"Okay. I need some time to digest all this, Wally. I never expected to be in the middle of a murder enquiry."

Bill departed from Wally's office and made his way to the nearest bar to think over what he had discussed with both Hugo and Wally. It occurred to him that he had not discussed with Wally what he went to talk about, but he would raise the subject of Sergeant Manning next time he met him.

The remains of Bill's house in Kensington were, at last, released by forensics.

Bill immediately put steps in hand to have the rubble removed and after about a week all that was left was a hole in the ground where the basement had been, between the neighbouring two properties.

Bill and Elle held several meetings, at various times, with reps from the local authority, builders and insurers. The builders obtained a house plan of the existing structure from the local authority, and after much toing and froing approval was eventually given for Bill's new home to be built.

The building insurers, however, were dragging their feet on release of any money because there was some discussion as to whether the house had been damaged by a deliberate act, as opposed to an accident. With no-one to put the finger on they at first intimated that the fire *could* have been started by Bill, so they elected to put the claim on hold until a perpetrator was found by the police. In any event, removal of the debris wasn't something covered by the insurance policy, so the insurers flatly refused to pay for this. House insurance was something that Bill would have to deal with later because he had other things to concentrate on.

The car insurers gave approval for a new car to be delivered to Bill's office. This was a great help because Brad was beginning to chivvy about the employees not having a run-around for various work activities, so the firm's car was returned by Bill.

On top of all this, the office refurbishment was completed, and the firm moved back into its home base. Bill was, again, offered the flat until his new home had been built, but he declined this on the basis that he could continue to stay at the manor, for now.

Despite frequent phone calls to Wally, the police still hadn't identified hoody, but wally's photo lab chaps were almost in a position to show his face. They were not quite there yet. Wally's investigation was ongoing, so Bill just had to leave him to it for the time being.

Chapter 20

March 2023.

It is now seven months since Amy's death and the police still had no leads. Bill knew that Wally was putting everything into solving the case, but '…*These things take time,*' he kept being told.

His friendship with Mel, at the tearoom, had developed into a strong bond between them. Whenever Bill returned to the office, he took Mel with him and Elle could see, from their body language, that the two were devoted to each other.

One afternoon in the cafe, while Bill sat at his usual table munching his lunch, Mel came to sit with him.

"Everything okay?" she asked.

"Of course. Since when have you ever given me a meal that is not okay?" he joked.

"I'm not talking about the food."

Bill looked up from his plate and studied Mel's face for a clue about what she meant.

Mel took a breath and asked Bill a question he didn't really want to be asked. "Where are we at, Bill? Where are we going with this relationship?"

"I… I don't know. Where do you think it's going?"

For the first time she said those immortal words, "I love you, Bill, but you never let me know how you feel."

"Mel, I know this bond we have between us is a strong one. A bond that will stand the test of time, but I don't think I'm ready to fully commit right now. Amy's memory is still with me and, as much as I want to be with you, I sometimes feel that I'm cheating on her. That's why I haven't tried to seduce you."

"It's been seven months, Bill. Don't get me wrong, I think you should always remember the times you had with Amy, and I will never take those memories away from you. But you must try to move on from Amy's death because until you do, you'll never be able to rebuild your own life. Elle thinks the same as I do."

"Oh, I get it. Ganging up on me, are you?" asked Bill with a wry smile. He pushed his plate away from him.

"No, of course not, but we both want what we think is best for you."

"I know. I just don't know what to do."

They looked into each other's eyes for what seemed like an eternity. It was abundantly clear to them both that they were very much in love and Mel knew that Bill just needed a push in the right direction.

She stood up from the table, walked over to the door and reversed the 'Open' sign. Walking back to the table she took Bill's hand and led him upstairs. He went without a fight...

At five p.m. Mel woke with a start. Someone was hammering on the cafe door.

Quickly pushing on some jeans, a top and some shoes she dashed downstairs to open the door. Facing her was a queue of people waiting to enter the cafe.

"When do you open?" asked the woman at the front of the queue.

Mel looked past the queue to see a small twelve-seater coach parked up on the kerbside. These people were obviously out-of-towners who had stopped for a break in their journey. It had begun to rain, and they all looked a bit bedraggled.

Reversing the 'Closed' sign and opening the door wide, Mel beckoned the queue into the cafe and went to the kitchen to don an apron.

Bill had, by now, risen from the bed and got dressed. Bouncing down the stairs he entered the cafe and smiled his best smile as he collected his half-eaten plate of lunch and took this to the kitchen. On the way he told the party of customers, "Won't be a minute. We're just putting the kettle on."

Entering the kitchen, he picked up Mel's pad and pencil and pointed to the kettle as he went back out to take orders. Mel laughed to herself as he blew her a kiss. She was impressed by the way Bill had taken charge of the impromptu situation and she busied herself preparing the utensils for when he returned with the orders.

When the visitors had departed, and all the crockery had been put in the dishwasher Mel took Bill in her arms and they kissed a long and passionate kiss.

Looking round, she said, "You're good at this."

In his usual jovial manner, Bill responded, "Yeah, and I'm not a bad waiter, either."

Chapter 21

Gloriana Rose Cottage

On returning to Colbert's Field Bill stood in front of the manor and looked across at the cottages.

He saw Charlotte waving to him, so he walked up to Iceberg Rose Cottage and looked up at her leaning out of the window.

"Where've you been?" she asked. "I've missed you."

"Oh, I've been a bit busy in London. How are you? Okay?"

"Yeah, I'm fine," she smiled.

Bill didn't ask if bully was around. He took that for granted on the basis that Charlotte wouldn't be chatting with him if bully was anywhere in the vicinity.

"You look better than you did the last time I saw you," declared Bill.

"Oh, then," she said, a frown appearing on her face. "I didn't want you to see me like that… After he had had his way with me. I'm sorry."

"Don't apologise. It wasn't your fault. You looked great just before that happened," smiled Bill.

"Do you want me to pose again?" she asked with a laugh on her face.

"I'd love you to," confirmed Bill, "but I've got to pick up some stuff and get going."

"Oh well. Maybe next time."

They heard the clang of the entrance gates down at the bridge being slammed shut and Charlotte quickly ducked back inside her cottage. They both thought it was bully returning for his fix of Charlotte humiliation.

Bill headed across the courtyard towards the manor. As he walked past Gloriana Rose Cottage he stopped in front of one of its windows because he saw movement out of the corner of his eye. Looking through the rose bordered window he saw an old lady, sat gently stroking the cat in her lap in front of a hearty blaze in the fireplace.

Bill almost knocked on her door to introduce himself but seeing the idyllic look on her face he thought, *'Better not disturb her.'* There may be a time for introductions in the future ... If he is still in the manor.

Remembering that bully might be on his way, he hurried across the courtyard back to the manor, glancing round furtively at the same time to make sure bully was nowhere to be seen. Nothing.

After entering the manor, he went straight upstairs to pack a few things to take back to London.

Picking up the telescope he zeroed in on the old woman's window. She was dozing in her chair. He then noticed some movement in the hallway. Panning over he saw a blonde-haired youth, about 18 years of age, skulking in the entrance hallway. Panning back to the old lady's front room he watched as she got up from her chair and went over to open the lounge door. As soon as she saw the youth she immediately walked back to stand in front of her chair, followed by the youth.

He watched as the old woman and the youth started a dialogue between them and it crossed Bill's mind that perhaps the youth was related to the woman. Perhaps her grandson, or maybe a nephew.

The woman reached up to her mantlepiece and took down a rare Wedgwood Fairyland Lustre "Geisha/Angels" patterned octagonal bowl. Bill had seen this standing on the mantlepiece and reflected on its high value. Reaching inside she took out a wad of rolled up bank notes and handed them to the youth.

Bill spoke to himself. "Oh yea..., some low-life relative scrounging off the old lady for some cash to buy drugs, no doubt."

He watched as more dialogue took place between the two, then was taken by surprise as the youth grabbed the bowl and smashed it over the woman's head. She went down like a lead balloon.

Bill shouted "Oi!" Nobody looked in his direction.

He shouted again, "Oi! You!"

Still no response.

With the woman lying on the floor the youth took two paces back, then stepped forward to kick her head as if it was a football. He then hurriedly made his way towards the cottage door.

Bill dropped the telescope and dashed downstairs to apprehend the youth. As he emerged from the manor, he saw the youth dash into Pilgrim Rose Cottage. Chasing after him, Bill ran into the cottage and stopped dead inside the hallway, listening for any sound that the youth would make.

He looked in the downstairs rooms. Nothing. No sign of the youth. Taking a look outside the back door he saw nothing but darkness. With no sound coming from inside the cottage it was apparent that the youth had disappeared into the night. He closed and bolted the back door and returned to the hallway.

It occurred to him that the youth might be upstairs so Bill took a long look into each of the first-floor rooms and returned to the hallway. The place was empty. Devoid of all furniture carpets, curtains... everything. A shell of a space at both ground and first floor levels.

Inside the cottage, Bill was puzzled by its emptiness and felt a huge sadness descend upon him like a dark, black cloud as if the cottage was mourning the loss of its family. Unnerved by the desolate feeling that had permeated Bill's mind, and certain that the youth wasn't hiding anywhere, he decided to leave as quickly as he could.

He tried to look in on the old woman.

Her door was locked so he couldn't enter the cottage. Taking a look through the window he saw no sign of the woman in the lounge.

'Perhaps she was able to get up and had gone into the kitchen?' thought Bill.

He knocked on her door. No answer. He knocked louder. Still no answer so he rapped heavily. Still no answer.

Bill couldn't leave it at that. The old lady might me lying somewhere in the cottage, incapable of moving or helping herself. Worse, she may be unconscious.

Rather than force an entry Bill decided to drive down to the police station and report what he had seen. He was anxious to provide some assistance to the old lady, if she needed it, and the police are the ones to look into it.

Arriving at the police station, after breaking every motoring law in the book, he found it to be closed.

Now unable to do anything more, he phoned Wally's home number. Wally was none too pleased about being disturbed, but he listened to what Bill had to say.

"Okay, Bill. Can you leave it with me? I'll get on to the local force to find out if she's okay."

With that, the call was terminated, and Bill returned to the manor to await the arrival of the police. After sitting in his viewing chair for about an hour, waiting for a police car to arrive, he fell asleep.

At four-thirty the following morning Bill woke with a start. Looking round in a daze he remembered the events of the previous evening and looked out to Gloriana Rose Cottage. All the lights had been turned off and the place was in darkness. A gentle breeze washed over the courtyard, pushing the leaves into a pile in a corner of the courtyard wall.

'*Perhaps…,*' Bill thought, '*the police had called while I was asleep?*'

He decided to make further enquiries with Sergeant Manning later that day.

Chapter 22

After a few hours of disturbed sleep Bill swung his legs over the side of the bed, rubbed his eyes and made his way to the kitchen to re-light the Aga and boil some water for his bath. While he waited for the water to boil, he reflected on the previous twenty-four hour's events.

There was Mel.

It is now apparent that their relationship had moved to the next level, and he wondered just how far it was going. He loved Mel but it was impossible to get over Amy's death and he didn't want his continued feelings for Amy clouding things with Mel. He decided to give it some more time to see how things panned out with Mel.

Then there was Charlotte.

She clearly wanted a better relationship with Bill, but with bully in the way Bill couldn't see any headway being made in her direction. Anyway, she was a married woman, and it wasn't in Bill's nature to be a marriage breaker. He decided there and then that Charlotte was a no-go area, although he wouldn't complain if she put on another show for him.

And what about the old lady in Gloriana Rose Cottage?

He reminded himself to look in on her on his return to the field. First, he must see Sergeant Manning. Perhaps she is okay? Perhaps she was taken to hospital? Manning would answer those questions. Either way, Bill decided to try to track down the woman's relatives… They, at least, should know that she is vulnerable, and maybe they will take steps to help her move to somewhere safer. A place where they can keep an eye on her.

Deciding to give breakfast a miss, he went into the village to see what Manning had to say about last night. Arriving at the station he was greeted by a fresh-faced police constable. Manning, apparently, was '... out of town.' It struck Bill that either he was getting older, or policemen were getting younger.

Bill introduced himself.

"Good morning, Mr. Colbert." The young policeman almost sang his response in an overly cheerful way. Perhaps that was something he'd learned in police college? "Sergeant Manning has told me all about you."

'*What,*' Bill thought, '*had Manning told this guy all about me?*'

"Good morning, Constable. I've just come to make a brief enquiry about the old lady in Gloriana Rose Cottage. Is she okay?"

The constable pursed his lips and thought carefully about his response.

"... What about the lady, sir?"

"Is she all right? I put the call out to the police, last night, when I saw that she had been attacked."

"Er... I'm not sure what you mean, sir. I've just been brought in on a temporary basis, this morning, while Sergeant Manning is away."

"Oh, You probably haven't been told. Can you ask Sergeant Manning to give me a call when he returns, so that I can ask him about her?"

"Certainly, sir," answered the constable, making a few notes on the pad of paper in front of him. He watched Bill leave the station then picked up the telephone handset to make a call.

Bill decided to call in on Mel for a coffee, on his way to the rail station.

Mel was her usual chirpy self when Bill entered the cafe.

Despite there being several customers sitting at the tables she welcomed Bill with a long, passionate kiss. The customers all cheered and clapped when she eventually decided to release Bill from her arms. Curtseying to them, she sashayed into the kitchen to fetch Bill's coffee.

Bill sat at a table in the corner of the cafe. His favourite seat had already been taken.

"Missed you," volunteered Mel as she sat down next to him.

"Oh? Why's that. I only saw you yesterday."

"I know, but I still miss you. What have you been up to today?"

"I've just been to the police station to report an attack on an old woman."

"What! Who?"

"Don't know her name, but I saw it all through her window."

"Really? Did you see who attacked her?"

"Yeah. I chased him but he got away. I've just reported it."

"Wow! How is she?"

"Don't know, but I'm sure the police will catch him. I gave them a good description."

Mel stood and announced to everyone, "This guy's a hero!" to lots more cheering and clapping.

Having finished his coffee, Bill said his goodbyes to Mel and went to catch a train to London. He promised Mel he would return the same night.

Back in London, he called into his office to drop off some work. He decided that at the same time he could sort out some more stuff for his refurbished office.

Entering the office, he was greeted by his secretary who informed him that Wally had phoned.

"I'll call him later today when I'm ready to leave here," Bill advised.

Picking up his mail and messages he made his way to his office. Brad was sat at his desk.

"Hiya, Brad. How's things?"

"Wally's been chasing you, and we had a Sergeant Manning call in to see you."

"Oh? I've been trying to contact him. Did he say what he wanted?"

"Nope, Just that he asked if you can see him, some time."

"Will do. I've brought back a few reports to amend and release. Julie's got some more on her desk that I'll pick up on my way out."

"No problems. Bill... are you okay?"

Bill looked at Brad with a puzzled face, trying to determine what he was asking.

"I'm... Fine. Why do you ask?"

"Well, Elle says she hasn't heard from you for ages. You go off to live in some undiscovered inherited manor house that you rarely speak of, a policeman calls to speak to you, you don't answer any calls to your mobile, Wally is anxious about you, and you've stopped letting people know where you are or what you're doing."

"I didn't know that I had to account for my every move. Nobody told me that when I came to work here," responded Bill, contrarily.

"Don't be like that, Bill. We're all worried about you."

"Well, there is no need to be. I'm fine. I'm just in the middle of something, that's all."

"Is it anything we can help with?"

"Look, stop clucking like a hen and just let me deal with this my way, will you?"

"Okay," answered Brad holding his hands up in submission. "Just tell me if you need anything. We've been friends for too long to have secrets, Bill, and I'd hate it if anything happened to you that we could have helped with."

"If I need you, I'll shout."

Bill left the office in a downbeat mood. What with everything that's happened at Colbert's field, involvement with Mel, Manning's apparent disbelieving attitude, Wally's report on the fire at his place and the Coroner's report on Amy's death it seemed, to Bill, that his whole world was caving in on itself.

He went to the bar, again, to do some more mulling over. Perhaps a stiff drink will help him think.

Chapter 23

Bill woke up with a start after being pushed on the shoulder.

His eyes looked like two tomatoes, the inside of his skull felt like it needed to explode, and his tongue felt like a hotel carpet. His breath had definitely been sautéed in stagnant pond water and his mouth was as dry as a Sahara sand dune.

Elle's voice invaded his eardrums like a carnival tannoy, echoing through millions of speakers.

"Time to wake up."

Squinting against the light he sat up and began to focus on his surroundings.

"Where the hell am I?" he croaked. His vocal cords were more like a ship's mooring ropes than violin strings, and he let out a hoarse cough to wake them up and get them vibrating properly.

"You're at my place," said Elle.

"How did I get here?"

"You apparently had a row with Brad and then disappeared, so Brad and I trolled through the bars to find you."

Bill just groaned.

"We found you at Mace's bar at about two a.m., asleep with your head on a table. The bartender had decided that it was safer to keep you there, rather than let you drunkenly wander about outside. We *eventually* got you into Brad's car and we brought you back here."

"Yeah, thanks for that. I do recollect the barman taking the bottle from my hand before I crashed out."

Elle brought him a cup of coffee that Bill drained in one go. She went to fetch another.

"What's wrong, Dad. It's not like you to go off the rails like this. What can we do to make life better for you?"

"Don't you start. I had that from Brad yesterday... Was it yesterday? What day is it?"

"You need to shower and change into some clean clothes. You've heaved up all over yourself, and my carpet, and you stink like a horse's arse."

Bill collected his jacket, felt in his pocket to confirm that his wallet was still present and left Elle's flat. He would need to enter his office flat via the emergency stairs to avoid any colleagues.

Whilst showering, he remembered that Sergeant Manning had called to see him. Perhaps it would be courteous for him to go to Manning's station to see what he wanted? He phoned the station and spoke to Manning, confirming that he was on his way and will meet him in about an hour.

Arriving at the police station in Colbert village, the sergeant instructed the young PC to watch the desk and escorted Bill to an interview room. He left Bill there for about five minutes while he went to brew a pot of tea.

"Thank you for coming in, Mr. Colbert. I just have a couple of questions to ask, then you can be on your way."

"Okay."

Opening the file in front of him the policeman studied its contents for a second, then looked up to face Bill.

"When you came here, and spoke to my young PC, you mentioned the old lady in Gloriana Rose Cottage."

"Yes, that's correct. I saw what happened and telephoned Inspecter Coombes to ask him to send reinforcements. I chased the perpetrator, but he escaped. I told the Inspector all about it."

Manning stared at Bill with a look of puzzlement on his face.

"We didn't get that call, at least not here at this station. I have, however, spoken to Inspector Coombes on several occasions prior to your visit."

Bill felt more perplexed than annoyed that Wally had not done anything about his call for help. A question suddenly sprang to his mind, unexpectantly, and bit him.

'What did happen to the old lady?'

He remembered seeing the cottage in darkness, all its lights turned off.

'Who turned the lights off?'

Bill resolved to find the answers to these questions when he returned to the manor.

Sergeant Manning continued his questioning. For some reason this session, to Bill's mind, seemed to have turned into an interrogation.

"What time did you see all this?"

"It was in the evening, some time. I don't recall, exactly. I know I woke up at about four-thirty the following morning and everything was quiet, so it must have been before then."

"And you telephoned for assistance then?"

"No, I telephoned after I chased the intruder and returned to the manor."

"I've got the notes, here, that the Inspector wrote when you phoned him," turning over a page. "You say the intruder was about five feet nine inches tall, wearing blue jeans, a denim top, sneakers and a bobble hat with blonde hair poking from underneath it." More a repeat of Bill's description than a question.

"Yes, that's right."

"And you say you saw this man kick the lady while she was on the floor?"

"Yes, what's all this about, Sergeant?"

"Well, sir. I'm just following up on my enquiries. I think you've answered all the questions that I had. Shall I show you out?"

Manning stood and opened the door for Bill to leave.

"What happened to the old lady? Is she okay?"

"It's still under investigation, sir. We'll let you know if we hear anything."

"What about the assault I reported? What's happened about that?"

"Still looking into it, sir."

With that, Bill left the station with more questions than he had answers to. He made his way to the tearoom.

Mel greeted him with her usual barrage of kisses and hugs.

"What happened to you? I thought you were coming back here the other night?"

"Oh, sorry. Something cropped up and I had to chase back to London. I should have let you know, but I forgot."

"No problem. Your loss, not mine," she said, with a cheeky smile on her face.

She continued, "You know that old woman you told me about? Well, I've been thinking. She wasn't the old woman that was murdered in one of those cottages on Colbert's Field, was she?"

Bill perked up. Here was someone who believed him.

"Yes, she was."

Mell looked puzzled. "How did you see it? She died ages ago.!"

Bill was stunned. He'd definitely witnessed the attack a couple of nights ago, so what did Mel mean?

"Well, I definitely saw it," responded Bill.

"Have it your way," said Mel dismissively, and she went to prepare Bill's lunch.

After lunch Bill returned to the manor.

Before going inside, he looked around at the cottages. They all stood with their windows looking at him, judgementally. He decided to look in on the old lady to find out if she was okay.

Her cottage door was still locked so Bill peered through a downstairs window. Surprisingly, the cottage was empty. No curtains, no carpets, no furniture, no pictures on the wall, no cat purring away in front of the old woman's rocking chair. Totally empty.

Bill thought to himself, *'didn't take them long to empty this place … It only happened a couple of days ago'*

Turning to Pilgrim Rose Cottage, he looked into its rose bordered window. Still empty, just like the last time he saw it.

Bill was now beginning to doubt whether he really had seen the incident when the old woman was attacked.

But the vision of her being kicked by the youth was such a vivid memory …

Chapter 24

May 2023

The best part of April and May were quiet at the manor. Bill restarted his weekday life of going to the cafe for breakfast with Mel, then on the train to London for work. This routine helped him forget about the goings on in the cottages; not even Charlotte made an appearance. With his thoughts settling down to more domestic matters, he returned to his task of cleaning up the rooms of the manor. Elle persisted in asking for an invite, but Bill just persisted in rebuffing her, "… until the place is a little tidier." At the weekends he had taken up his favourite hobby of fishing, spending many hours of spring sunshine lounging by the trout stream, occasionally catching a decently sized trout to cook for tea that evening.

Whilst in the office, one morning, Elle came in to pass the time of day.

"Have you finished sorting your stuff out, yet?" she asked.

This conversation reminded him that he still had Amy's possessions in a box in a cupboard. The box that Bill had extracted from her workplace. Elle persuaded him that it was time to decide what to keep out of this assortment of articles. She was right, of course. Down-to-earth Elle had been Bill's rock while he got over Amy's death and she had always steered him in a good direction whenever he felt down.

They sat at the coffee table and gradually emptied the box. The picture with its broken frame was put to one side while stuff that was no good to anyone else - shoes, a scarf, a hat, a spare pair of slacks and spare underwear - were consigned to the waste bin, unless Elle expressed a wish to keep something. The box also contained Amy's more intimate stuff. Her handbag, her mobile phone, her diary and a small notebook. These were put to one side while Bill and Elle explored Amy's handbag. The usual stuff that women hide away in their bags was immediately consigned to the bin. You know, stuff like tissues, combs, hairbrush, make-up, pills and a used hanky. As soon as the box was empty Bill tipped the contents of the waste bin into it. He would dump this stuff in the large wheelie bin located in the car park later, on his way out of the office. Elle decided to keep the tote bag and handbag.

Of interest to Bill were the only three items left on the table; Amy's diary, her notebook and her mobile phone.

Bill tried to turn on the phone. The battery was dead, so he extracted his own charging cable from his desk and plugged the phone into a nearby wall socket.

He and Elle explored the notebook while the phone took up enough charge to enable Bill to open it. Flicking through the pages of it they didn't find anything of interest to them. The entries were mostly about work related matters... Reminders to take a report, or update a chart or talk to someone, etc. One entry, however, jumped out of the page at them. It was a one-liner to remind Amy to discuss 'M' with Bill. This had been crossed out, as if Amy had changed her mind about discussing 'M' with Bill.

There was no date with the note to provide a time when the reminder was made, but it was tucked in between a collection of notes written around June or July of last year, 2022.

The two people looked at each other. Who was 'M'? What did Amy want to discuss with Bill about him... Or her? Neither Bill nor Elle knew of any of Amy's friends with a name beginning with 'M'. This question was put on the back burner for now, but they both made a mental note to try to find out.

The diary posed a problem, initially, for Bill and Elle. Although Bill didn't keep a diary, Elle did. Not a hard copy like this one, but a digital copy on her laptop. They both discussed the pitfalls of reading someone else's private thoughts, particularly Amy's.

"You know, there's a lot of wisdom in the old adage *'What the eye doesn't see, the heart can't grieve over.'*" warned Bill. "Do we really want to delve into her private life, like this?"

There was a pause while Elle tried to think of an answer.

"You're right. I know I wouldn't want my secret thoughts to be aired, but what harm can it do to mum now?"

"I wasn't thinking about your mum. I was thinking more about us. Do we really want to know what she thought of both you, or I, or anyone else if it matters?"

At the back of their minds, both Bill and Elle recalled Elle's outburst about Amy having an affair.

Bill resurrected the conversation.

He counselled, "If she *was* having an affair, you know that it'll probably be mentioned here?" waving the diary in front of Elle. "Do we honestly want to drag this up and risk upsetting ourselves? Can't we just remember her as she was... Before you saw her with some bloke in the rail station?"

With a hint of tears in Elle's eyes, she answered, "Yeah, I suppose so. She's gone, anyway, so it doesn't matter what's in the diary."

Bill dropped the diary in the box for disposal.

They turned their attention to Amy's phone, now with sufficient battery power to boot up. Pressing the 'On' key they waited while the screen woke up. Swiping up to log on, nothing happened for about five seconds then the keypad popped up, waiting for a password.

"Damn. She's protected logon with the facial recognition system," Bill muttered.

"Let me try," Elle offered, holding the phone up to her face. "It's worth a try…"

Nothing.

"It's waiting for a password," volunteered Elle.

"Do you know it?" asked Bill.

"No, don't you?"

"Nope."

They looked into space while they tried to think of what Amy would use as a password. Elle came up with a suggestion. It didn't work. Bill came up with another suggestion. That didn't work, either.

"We're facing brick walls here," said Bill. "I'll get the phone to Wally to see if his guys can unlock it."

Elle looked at Bill and blew out a frustrated sigh. "It might have given us some idea of who she was meeting," she said.

Suddenly they both faced each other, eyebrows raised in surprised recall. Elle was the first to say what they were both thinking.

"The diary might tell us that…!"

For a brief moment they sat looking at each other, waiting to see who would make the first move. Both of them made for the box of rubbish at the same time.

Forgetting any notion that the contents of the diary might be painful to them, Bill and Elle started to flick through the diary's pages. Most of the stuff talked about

158

what Amy and Bill did, or what Elle had talked about to Amy. Private, intimate stuff. But neither Bill nor Elle took any notice of those thoughts, they were more interested in finding out who 'M' was.

Page after page turned up nothing of interest. Amy was meticulous in her recordings of work conversations, home amusements, mini disasters in her family's life, holiday events, Elle's disappointments, client conversations. She wrote memories of almost every minute of her life, from getting up in the morning to going to bed at night.

Bill and Elle were about to forget this idea when Elle noticed something that piqued their interest. It was an entry dated some time in August 2022, the day after Bill had flown out to Belgium for his meeting about the stolen stamps.

M arr. 2:30. He wants to talk about D &B.
I'll take his mind off the subject with some of the usual.
He'll come round to my way of thinking.

There he was … 'M'. It was clear that Amy didn't want to discuss 'D' or 'B'. Who was 'D'? David March? Who was 'B'? It had to be Bill. But who was 'M'? Was it 'M' as in David March? And *where*, precisely, was he arriving at?

These were questions that were difficult to answer at this stage, and this was the only reference to 'M' in the diary. It was unclear why. What was obvious was that Amy had had clandestine meetings with someone while Bill was away. Bill silently wondered how many other such meetings had Amy had with 'M'.

The following day Bill met up with Wally.

"Hiya, Bill. What have you got for me?"

Bill handed over Amy's phone. "Any chance you can get this unlocked for me on the QT? It's Amy's phone and I'm pretty sure we might be able to reveal who she might have let in that night."

"Sure. Is it just locked with a password?"

"Unfortunately, not. She seems to have enabled the facial recognition function."

"Well, I don't think it's impossible. I'll get one of my guys to look at it. Have you got a decent photo of her?"

"The only one I've got now is a photo she had at work. The rest were destroyed in the fire."

"If you can get that to me, I'll see what we can do."

"Talking of the fire, have you got any more info on who or why?"

"Nothing so far, but these things take time. I reckon *somebody* will come forward at some stage to give up a bit of knowledge, but we'll keep looking."

"That's good to know, Wally. Anything on hoody?"

"Nah, not a lot. You've seen what we've seen. We got a heads up on a 1986 Audi 5000S, parked a couple of streets away, but that lead has died on us."

"Mm… Might be worth remembering."

"Yea. While you're here, I got an odd visit from one of the regional sergeants a while ago. He wanted to know all about you."

"That would be Manning…" Bill was cut off from his sentence by Wally.

"He was asking me if you had a history with us. Did you take drugs. Any mental problems. That kind of thing."

"Ignore him, Wally. He's just a condescending prat. I reported a couple of incidents to his station, but nothing has been done. I've stopped talking to the guy. If I get anything else that's remotely iffy I'll call you if that's okay."

"No probs. It's just that I don't think he believes what you're telling him. He thinks that you know more than you're letting on."

Bill studied Wally's face for a moment, trying to see if Wally was just taking an interest, or if he was fishing for something else. He didn't answer the question.

"You gonna let me know about the phone?" asked Bill.

"Of course."

With that, Bill left Wally's office and made his way to Mel's place for a meal.

Chapter 25

Sunrise Rose Cottage

June 2023.

The spring sunshine of May turned into the balmy weather of June. The roses were in full bloom and the gardens took on the magical manicured look of a picture postcard. All the cottage windows had regained their rose bordered explosion of colour as the flowers opened up to absorb the sun's rays and allow the bees to drink their nectar. A pretty sight, and Bill wondered how such a beautiful place could harbour the evil goings on that he had witnessed.

Bill still hadn't seen anything of Charlotte. He thought that perhaps she had gone to stay with a relative for a while. Maybe her mother, or sister? Maybe she had decided to get away from bully for a while. *'A good call'* thought Bill, although a second thought occurred to him that perhaps he may have done something to put her in hospital… Or worse! Not that it had anything to do with Bill. He was just interested, that's all. Curiously, he had not seen anything of bully for a while, either. He took an occasional look through Charlotte's cottage window, but the furniture was still there so he was satisfied that she would return when she was ready.

His relationship with Mel had also moved on a pace. He spent a lot of his spare time at the cafe, helping to serve or clearing the tables, and when times were quiet, he and Mel disappeared upstairs for an hour or two. Occasionally, he took her to London so that she could do some window browsing and shopping and Bill's colleagues welcomed her warmly. Elle and Mel became good friends.

Elle continued to press Bill for a visit to the manor and Bill continued to decline, and Mel continued to press him to leave the manor and Bill also continued to decline. When he eventually got round to installing a proper gas boiler and running hot water perhaps that would be a good time to have a housewarming party. For the time being, however, he will make do with his bathtub down in the kitchen.

On his way back to the manor, one day with an armful of reports to check, he was brought to an abrupt stop in the courtyard. He saw his mysterious shadow duck behind the bedroom curtain. The same shadow that he saw when he first went to the manor. Was it a shadow, or was it a trick of the light? Dumping the reports on the kitchen worktop he cautiously climbed the staircase until he was outside his bedroom door. Slowly opening the bedroom door, he peered inside to find … Nobody there. He thoroughly searched every room in the manor to see if anyone had entered it while he was away, but nothing. Nobody anywhere in the manor. Perhaps it was, indeed, a trick of the light.

With a shrug of his shoulders, he went back down to the lounge to get on with his report checking. Brad had, again, tackled him about his present work ethos, this time complaining. He was getting irritated that Bill was not, in his eyes, "… pulling your weight in terms of sharing the load of travelling to the client's locations." Bill felt a little guilty about this and promised to give more thought to his role in the partnership. He was, however, torn between making more of an effort, workwise, or spending more time with Mel. For the time being he would continue to check reports.

That afternoon he decided that the weather was too nice to miss out on a bit of fly fishing and he went to the stream to relax. After an hour or two he packed his catch up in a clean tea towel and made his way back to the manor to prepare the trout for his evening meal.

Walking up the hill he noticed a young lady kneeling in the front garden of Sunrise Rose Cottage, tending the roses. She looked to be about 18 years old, and she was wearing a striking gold top with sequins that shimmered in the summer sun. She was attractive, with a shock of dark brown hair and smile that any film director would kill for. He smiled and waved to her. She smiled and waved back. Not wishing to intrude, Bill made his way to the manor and disappeared inside, thinking, '*I've not seen her before. Perhaps she's just visiting?*'

After a satisfying meal of grilled trout, new potatoes, peas and cabbage he washed up and tidied the kitchen and went up to bed for an early night. Although it was still light outside, the fishing trip had tired him, and it was a good opportunity to get some uninterrupted sleep.

Undressing in the dark he saw the door of Sunrise Rose Cottage open. The young lady appeared from within. She turned and spoke to someone inside the cottage before shutting the cottage door. With a smile on her face, she casually walked down the path and stood outside her gate, breathing in the warm summer air. Slowly strolling towards the bridge over the stream she seemed to be in a world of her own, gently stroking the roses as she passed them. Occasionally, with her nose inside a flower's delicate petals, she inhaled its scent before resuming her walk. Bill could almost feel the happiness oozing from her.

A movement in some bushes the lady had just passed caught his eye. With one eye on the bush and the other on the lady Bill silently watched from his window, wondering if the movement was just the summer breeze blowing the rose stems to wave the flowers at him. As the lady disappeared from sight, someone appeared from the bush. Concentrating on the person, now walking with some purpose in the direction of the lady, Bill could see that it was definitely male, and it was definitely the same youth that he saw kicking the old woman in Gloriana Rose Cottage a few months ago.

He dashed downstairs three or four at a time and rushed out of the manor as quickly as his legs would take him. Once in the courtyard he looked in the direction of the youth and saw him running, as if he was trying to catch up with the young lady. Bill ran in hot pursuit, thinking that he would now have the opportunity of apprehending the youth. With the bridge in sight, he heard the young lady scream, "Help!". Bill continued his charge towards the bridge and heard another anguished cry. "No …! Stop …! No, Arrrgh!" Spurred on by the lady's petrified screaming Bill dashed across the bridge and found … Nothing! The night air was as still and as silent as graveyard.

It was now quite dark, but Bill spent a good half hour searching the lane and hedgerows. Nothing. He knew *something* had happened to the young lady, and he knew that the youth had been involved, but he didn't know what. He took his phone out of his pocket and phoned Wally.

"You'd better get some men out here, Wally. I think I may have witnessed another assault." Bill went on to describe the evening's events.

"Another one?" answered Wally, incredulously. "I'll get on to Sergeant Manning. He's a lot closer than me."

Thinking that Manning would probably regard this report with about the same seriousness as the others that he had made, Bill continued his search for another ten to fifteen minutes before deciding that it was too dark to carry on. With nothing to find, Bill thought to himself, *'There's little wonder that Manning doesn't believe me. There's never anything to find!'*

Much disheartened, and with his head bowed, Bill made his way back to the manor. He decided not to see Manning himself, tomorrow. He will wait to see what Manning will do.

Chapter 26

July 2023.

The remainder of June had passed without any further sightings from Bill's window.

He'd had more than a few restless nights, thinking about what he had witnessed from his window in the past, but it seemed that absolutely nobody believed him. In his own mind he definitely saw all the goings on, so why wasn't there any record of them. Surely, such vividly violent events *must* have been recorded by the police, but why hadn't Sergeant Manning looked into them in more detail. Maybe he had. Maybe it was police protocol to not share such information with the public. But if he *had* made further enquiries, why was he treating Bill as if he was an imbecile? As if Bill was the guilty party. And why didn't Manning share the information with Wally. Even Wally was beginning to act as if Bill was off his rocker.

Pushing these thoughts to the back of his mind, Bill decided to visit Mel. She was usually a good way of taking one's mind off one's troubles. Arriving at the cafe he saw the 'Closed' sign on the inside of the door, and the door locked. Perhaps she had gone to do some shopping somewhere. He called her from his mobile phone.

"Hiya, Mel. It's me."

"Hello, lover. What are you up to?"

"I'm outside the tearoom. I thought I would spend a bit of time with you."

"Sorry. Should have called earlier. I'm in London looking for some decent pans."

"Oh. Okay. See you some other time, then."

"Yep. I'll give you a call."

Conversation terminated; Bill stood looking around the village. Apart from the occasional couple entering or leaving a shop the town was as quiet as a mouse wearing slippers in a library.

'Perhaps Elle is free,' thought Bill. Raising his phone to his ear, once more, he waited until Elle answered.

"Hiya, Elle. It's only me. Are you free for some lunch?"

"Can't today, Dad. I'm on the way to Hull to meet up with the CEO of WealthyPeople Magazine. They're doing an article on recovery of stolen jewellery and have asked if we will provide some input. Another time, perhaps?"

"Yeah, okay."

Another conversation terminated.

Bill knew that Brad was in Europe, somewhere, chasing down a diamond tiara, so he would be no good for a meet-up, and he didn't want to disturb Wally from his busy itinerary. There was only one thing to do... Have a quiet day fishing.

On his way back to the manor Bill called into the local corner shop to buy a couple of bottles of wine. If Mel was going to call him for a meet-up, the least he could do is to be prepared for one of Mel's multi-course meals. With a basket in the crook of his arm he chose the wine and added a bottle of whiskey.

Arriving at the checkout counter he put the basket down, unloaded its contents and waited for the cashier to calculate how much he owed.

While she waited for him to retrieve and delve into his wallet, the cashier asked, "Are you the gentleman that owns Colbert's Field?"

"Yes," answered Bill with a little suspicion in his voice.

"You're not going to build houses on it, are you?"

'What is it with these people about not building houses on that field?' Bill thought.

"No, I'm not going to build any houses on that field. Why?"

"Oh, it's such a pretty field. It would be a shame to spoil it."

Having paid for his booze, Bill left the shop with a puzzling thought.

'That's the third time I've been asked that. What are these people worried about?'

He made his way back to the manor. On his way the sky turned a charcoal colour and without any warning the heavens opened up and poured non-stop rainwater onto the village and its surrounding fields. Bill was drenched by the time he reached the manor and he resigned himself to the fact that fishing was off, for today.

Approaching the courtyard, he looked up at his bedroom window. He had got into the habit of doing this each time he returned to the manor. On several occasions he had seen a mysterious shadow duck behind the window reveal when he approached the building. Despite dashing upstairs to see if anyone had entered the manor unannounced, he always found nothing, and this now puzzled him.

There it was, again! It was as if the shadow wanted to be seen but had changed its mind and decided that it did not want to be seen. Bill wasn't going to dash upstairs this time to find an empty room. He had made his mind up that it was just an anomaly. A reflection of a car passing by, perhaps, or maybe a reflection of the sun from one of the cottage windows. Oddly, though, he'd seen this shadow at a time when the sun was behind the clouds, or in the evening when there was no sun.

With his clothes saturated from the pouring rain he put a pan of water on the Aga to boil for a bath, lit the gas, stripped off in the kitchen and sat in the lounge in his dressing gown. Before picking up another boring report to check he decided to open one of the bottles of wine. He forgot about the pan of water waiting to boil on the Aga hob.

Without realising it, both bottles of wine were drained, and half of the whiskey had been drunk.

Actually, 'drunk' is the operative word, here, because Bill was most definitely drunk. Head spinning, eyes finding it difficult to focus, legs unable to support him, Bill rested his head on the arm of the settee... *'Just for a couple of minutes.'* It didn't even take one minute for him to succumb to the darkness of a drunken slumber.

It was dark when Bill heard someone calling his name. As much as he didn't want to, he gingerly opened one eye to peer through the mist of hangover to see who was calling him. Nothing but darkness. Perhaps he could keep his eyes closed for just another few minutes. Enough time to pull himself together and open his eyes properly. Then he heard his name being called again.

"Bill... BILL, WAKE UP!"

With a jolt he opened his eyes and lifted his head from the arm of the settee. A hammer thumped out an echo on the inside of his skull. Holding his head in his hands he sat up. This was one hell of a hangover. The worst one he had experienced for a long time. Again, he heard his name being called.

"Bill. Over here."

Startled, he looked round. The room was in darkness, but he could just about make out the shape of the furniture and the door and window letting the bright moonlight in through its aged panes. Rubbing his forehead in the hopes that that would ease the thumping going on inside his head he looked around once more.

"Bill. Look at me," pressed the voice inside his head. "Concentrate."

Now fully awake he could think a little bit straighter than when he first woke up. Peering into the darkness by the window he saw a wisp of smoke. No, it wasn't smoke. It was a shape. A see-through shape in a transparent human form… What appeared to be a person, but not a real person. A person behind what seemed to be a shimmering cloud, similar to the heat haze in a desert.

Bill sat there, staring at this unearthly form, trying to focus properly from behind the shroud of his hangover. As his focus improved, he could clearly see a face. A woman's face. He shook his head as if that would bring his reality back to the present, but the ghostly shape just smiled and drifted closer to him.

"Bill," he heard. "Bill, don't be afraid. I need you to listen carefully."

Bill's jaw dropped and he sat with an open mouth, trying to comprehend what was happening. He could now make out all the features on the face peering out of the cloudy mist, and he was rooted to the spot, stuck in a world between worlds. The face was that belonging to Amy!

"You're not real …" Bill said, as much to himself as to the apparition in front of him. "I'm still asleep. I'm dreaming."

The apparition smiled.

"You must listen to me."

"Is that you, Amy? Nooo… You're dead…"

"Bill, listen to me," with some urgency.

Bill sat back and waited for what seemed like an eternity before finding the courage to speak up.

"What? What do you want?" he asked, not believing that he was actually speaking to an uninvited apparition.

"Elizabeth is in grave danger, but you must not worry. I'll help her."

"What...? I... What do you mean? My Elizabeth? Elle?"

"Yes, Elizabeth. She is going to need my help."

"What danger? What do I have to do?" questioned Bill.

"Sleep now, I'll help Elle but be ready to go to her," the apparition said, then slowly sank back into the darkness and disappeared.

The next thing Bill knew was that the brightness and warmth of the sun shining through the window had stirred him from his slumber. It was seven a.m. in the morning.

After opening his eyes, he lay there, trying to figure out what he had seen during the night.

Had he seen anything? Had he interacted with an apparition? An apparition that had Amy's face and soft inviting voice? Was it a dream? It seemed more like a nightmare.

Bill then noticed that he didn't have a hangover. Still wearing his dressing gown, he was as fresh and as wide awake now as if he'd just had the best night's sleep he had ever had. He felt young again, and alive, eager to face the day.

With a start, he remembered about the pan of water he had put on the Aga hob the previous night. It will have boiled dry by now and probably have melted the pan overnight. Dashing into the kitchen he found the pan sitting on the floor, still full of water. The Aga fire had died to grey embers. He was sure he put the pan on the hob before settling down with the reports… But maybe not? He tried to recollect the night's events, but all he could remember was that he had got drunk.

He shrugged his shoulders and thought to himself *'Yeah. It was all just a dream. A realistic and vivid dream, but a dream, nonetheless. It couldn't be anything else… could it?'*

Chapter 27

Alaska Rose Cottage

It was difficult for Bill to shrug off the image that he saw last night.

As he dressed, he thought of the words that he thought he heard the apparition say.

'Elizabeth is in danger…'

'… I'll help her.'

'Be ready…'

Pensively, he sat in his 'viewing' chair in his underpants and shirt and looked out of the window.

The words resonated around the inside of his head like a ball bouncing off walls.

Although he was still convinced it was all a dream, he thought it better to be safe, and he stabbed Elle's number onto his phone keypad. After a couple of rings, she answered.

"Hi Dad. You're nice and early today."

"Yeah. Woke up early."

"Oh? Got a problem?"

"Not really. Are you okay?"

"Course I am. Why?"

"Oh, nothing. Just thought I'd call to see how you are. That's all."

"Well, I'm fine. Are you coming in today? We could have some lunch."

"Sounds like a plan. What time?"

"About one-thirty? Usual place?"

"Magic!"

Disconnecting the call, he sat back in the knowledge that Elle was as cheerful as ever and, more importantly, safe. His love for Elle knew no bounds and since Amy had died the bond between them had grown stronger. Bill would brave hell and high water to protect her.

As he sat looking out of the window, he caught sight of bully exit from Iceberg Rose Cottage and furtively creep across to Alaska Rose Cottage. Giving the door a quiet knock, he stood there, looking back at Iceberg as if checking to see if he was being watched. He was, most definitely, being watched. Bill could see Charlotte hiding behind a curtain, peeking through a gap between this and the window reveal.

The door to Alaska Rose opened and Bill watched as bully was invited in.

Bill thought back to the time that he had first met Charlotte. That was way back in November, last year. They met down at the trout stream.

He recalled that she had once jokingly told him to "… *keep an eye on Alaska Rose Cottage. You'll be surprised at what you see.*"

Actually, knowing what he now knows about bully he wasn't surprised at all. Assuming, of course, that some sort of illicit liaison was taking place. It was none of Bill's business, so he finished dressing and made his way to Mel's place for breakfast.

The bell over the cafe door jingled as Bill opened it and he was immediately confronted by a mass of about thirty people queuing at the counter. They had obviously disembarked from the coach parked outside the cafe and Bill could see that Mel was rushed off her feet.

Excusing himself past the queue he stood behind the counter, raised his palms and called, "Please take a seat and I'll come and get your orders."

The customers spread out to the waiting tables, chattering excitedly amongst themselves.

Mel smiled at Bill, gave him a peck on the cheek and disappeared into the kitchen. Bill retrieved the pad and pen from a drawer and started his rounds, writing orders furiously and passing these through the serving hatch to Mel.

At about nine thirty the place was in total silence, the group of tourists having finished and paid for their breakfasts and boarded their bus to wherever they were travelling to.

Bill and Mel enjoyed their own breakfasts as they sat and chatted at Bill's favourite table. The couple Bill had met when he first arrived at Colbert's Village saw them both through the cafe window and waved to them. The woman turned to her companion and whispered something that made them smile broadly and turn back to wave, once more, to Bill.

'I wonder if they know about us?' Bill thought to himself.

Bill gave Mel a fond smile and thought, *'Do we care?'*

'Not in the least,' he decided.

After clearing away the dishes, wiping all the tables down and helping Mel with the washing up Bill left the cafe to make his way back to the manor. He still had a stack of reports to plough through before meeting Elle for lunch.

Approaching the courtyard, he saw bully remonstrating with another man in front of Alaska Rose Cottage. The woman from the cottage stood looking out of her open door as she propped up the doorframe, tears running down her cheeks. From the heated conversation that Bill heard, the man confronting bully was the woman's husband. It was clear that he had returned home unexpectedly to find bully and the woman in his home.

Bill stopped and watched the fracas, arms folded across his chest.

Bully and the man started to fight. A disorganised, scrappy fight when nobody landed a serious punch. The woman lunged forward to try to part the two men, but she was cruelly punched by bully, and she dropped to the ground. This infuriated the husband further and he picked up a rock and hurled it at bully. It glanced off bully's head as he turned from punching the woman and, roaring like an enraged bull he charged at the husband, knocking him backwards and landing a hefty punch on the husband's cheek. The husband dropped to the ground like a bag of washing and laid there as bully kicked his head with blow after blow. With blood oozing from the husband's ears, nose and mouth the woman picked herself up and lunged once more at bully. She received another punch to her face and bully returned to kicking the husband.

Bill shouted "Oi!" and moved forward to stop the kicking. As he stood in front of bully, ready to plunge into him to stop the kicking, bully stepped back and glared at Bill. An evil, gnarled glare that bared his nicotine-stained teeth, spittle drooling from the sides of his mouth, his eyes wide with anger and blood lust. For just a fraction of second, Bill thought he recognised bully's face behind the contorted mask of evil intent, but the thought left Bill's head in a flash as he looked at the raging bull confronting him. Bill raised his fists, ready to fend off the animal in front of him but bully just turned and walked back to Iceberg Rose Cottage. Bill saw Charlotte looking out of her bedroom window.

Turning back to look at the woman, she was kneeling over her husband, crying.

She looked up at Bill and moaned, "He's dead!"

Stunned, Bill hurriedly said to the woman, "Don't touch him. I'll phone the police." He dialled 999 but got no signal, just white noise.

In a panic Bill shouted, "Wait there. Don't touch him!" as he turned and started his run to the police station. On his way he tried phoning Sergeant Manning, but his call went to white noise again.

The station was closed and locked up. Bill took out his phone and called Wally. This time he managed to get a decent signal.

"Wally," he declared, breathing heavily, "I've just witnessed a murder. Get somebody down here now!"

"Whoa, Bill. Calm down and tell me what happened."

Bill explained what he had just witnessed.

Wally took a moment to write down a few details then asked Bill, "Now, you're sure this happened at the field?"

"Yes, yes. I'm outside the police station but there's nobody here. The woman needs help now."

"All right, all right. I'll get onto the local force. Stay where you are."

"I'm going back to help the woman."

"No! Don't do that. This bloke sounds too dangerous for you to be anywhere near him. I'll phone somebody."

"But the woman needs some urgent medical attention, She's been beaten."

"Do not go back there, Bill," shouted Wally, "I mean it! I don't want you contaminating the scene."

Wally calmed his voice and suggested that Bill goes to the cafe for a cup of coffee. "I'll get someone to come and see you," he promised.

Bill terminated the call. He was torn between returning to help the woman or doing what Wally had told him, by staying away from the scene. He decided that helping the woman was more important than preserving evidence. If, as Wally had suggested, someone from the local force was on their way it made no difference if the scene was contaminated by Bill because he had already contaminated it by confronting bully. Whoever was coming can come straight to the field. He made his way back to help the woman and also to possibly protect Charlotte.

Jogging along the road he noticed a column of smoke rising from the field. Increasing to a run he dashed through the gate, up the hill and stopped abruptly at the scene before him.

Alaska Rose Cottage was encased in flames that reached to the sky in total abandonment.

Bill ran to the courtyard, but he knew it was impossible to do anything to stem the flames. He looked round for the woman and her husband, but they were nowhere to be seen. Bill hoped to God that they were not inside the burning cottage, but at the back of his mind he knew they were.

He decided to do as Wally had instructed and wait at the cafe.

Chapter 28

Sat in the cafe, Bill was subdued. Mel had noticed his quiet manner but had decided against probing too far. She also noticed his dishevelled turnout, but she ignored it.

She went about her business of changing tablecloths and preparing food without disturbing Bill's engrossed thoughts.

After a period of worrying about him, she sat opposite him with two fresh mugs of coffee and waited for him to speak. Nothing. Bill just stared down at the bowl of sugar he was absentmindedly stirring with his teaspoon.

"What's wrong Bill?" she asked.

Bill looked up and smiled. "Nothing," he offered.

"Why so glum, then?" Mel probed.

"It's nothing," Bill replied, slightly annoyed at the questions and keeping his eyes down.

"Doesn't look like nothing. You've just sat there for a good twenty minutes and not said a word to me. You just sit staring at that bowl of sugar. What's wrong?"

"Look! It's something that I have to deal with. I don't want you to be any part of it. Okay?"

"No, it's not okay. I love you enough to care, but how can I care if you don't confide in me?"

Bill raised his head and looked into Mel's eyes. He saw tears welling up and he felt ashamed that he had upset her. His attention returned to the sugar. Mel stood up and disappeared into the kitchen, in a huff. She returned moments later and almost threw Bill's lunch plate on the table. Turning to angrily march back to the kitchen she was brought to an abrupt stop as Bill grabbed her apron. He stood to face her. As he held her to him, she sobbed into his chest. Bill took a serviette from the table, raised her chin with his index finger and started to wipe the tears from her cheeks.

With a smile he said, "Is this our first argument?"

Half laughing, half sobbing she looked at him, not knowing how to reply.

"Sit down and I'll explain," Bill said.

With both of them sitting and facing each other, Bill with his elbows supporting his chin and Mell using the serviette to blow her nose, Bill took a deep breath and spoke first.

"I'm sorry. I didn't realise that you were getting upset, and you're right. I should confide in you more."

Mell put down the serviette and replied, "I'm not being nosy. I really don't want to intrude on your private thoughts. I'm just concerned that you've got something on your mind that is upsetting you. I don't like seeing you this way, all quiet and moody and if there is anything I've done to upset you, you must say so."

Bill smiled a sympathetic smile. "It's not you, Mel. I promise. You know how much I love you and you know that I would never intentionally upset you but yes, I do have something on my mind. Something that bothers me but something that I think only I can deal with. I honestly don't want you upset by my problems."

Mel took Bill's hand and kissed it. "What is it?" she asked.

Bill sat back and paused for a moment, thinking of a way to tell Mel what his problem was.

The bell over the door chimed as the door was opened. They both looked in the direction of the door to see Sergeant Manning enter. Looking round, he spotted Bill and made a beeline towards his table.

Seeing Mel's tear-filled eyes he said, "Sorry to intrude. Am I interrupting something?"

Bill and Mel looked back at each other, and Mel answered. "It's nothing Sergeant. Shall I get you a coffee?"

"Yes, please. That would be great," the sergeant answered and sat down in the chair Mel had just vacated.

Manning sat in silence until the kitchen door swung shut behind Mel.

Looking Bill squarely in the face he said, "I've had another call from your mate in the Yard," referring to Wally.

"Oh yeah? What about?"

"About what you claim to have seen this morning."

"What about it?"

The conversation was in grave danger of spiralling to another standoff, but Manning spoke up. "Look Bill… Can I call you Bill?" Manning waited for a nod from Bill.

Mel had returned with Manning's coffee. She put the mug down in front of him and brought a chair to sit at the table with the two men.

Manning took a sip of his coffee. "Tastes good," he said to Mel before continuing his conversation with Bill.

"What are you doing here, Bill."

"I'm having a cup of coffee with Mel."

"No, why are you here, in Colbert Village? What do you want?"

"I don't want anything. I've inherited Colbert's Field and it's my right to go there. I haven't broken any laws. In fact, I've tried to abide by the law each time I reported something."

"No, you haven't broken any laws. But why are you dossing in the manor. Not even the crows like that place."

"None of your business. It's mine and I'll live in it as long as I want to."

Manning changed the subject. "Don't get me wrong, but are you sure you saw what you say you saw?"

"Yes. Of course, I'm sure. I wouldn't have said it if I wasn't sure."

"Okay, I'll take your word for it, but this is the fourth time you allege to have seen an incident of this type up on that field. Just tell me what happened this time."

"I've already given Wally a statement…" Bill was interrupted by Manning.

"Yes, sir, but I want to hear it from you direct."

Bill's look alternated between Manning and Mel.

He recalled the events of the morning to Manning, exactly as he had passed them on to Wally. When he had finished, he sat back to wait for Manning to comment. Manning blew out a large, long breath and leaned forward to speak to Bill.

"I'll take what you've just told me under advisement but in the meantime, Bill, I suggest you take a good long look at yourself and think about taking a rest from work for a while."

"What are you intimating?" asked Bill.

Looking at Mel, then Bill, Manning stood to depart from the cafe. Before doing so, he voiced a stern warning to Bill.

"This will be the last warning you get, Bill. Stop wasting police time. I don't know why you continue to make these allegations, but if you don't stop you will leave me with little alternative but to section you under the Mental Health Act. Do you understand?"

Bill jumped to his feet in defiance.

"What …? What …! How dare you insinuate such a thing," protested Bill, angrily.

Mel stood to calm him down but was unsuccessful. Bill continued to face Manning.

"You know what I think?" asked Manning calmly.

"No, but I'm confident that you're going to tell me."

"To be honest, Bill, I think you know more than you're letting on," Manning said.

Bill looked aghast and retorted, "I've reported three murders and a severe beating to the police and what have they done? Nothing … Absolutely nothing! Not you, Not your constable, not Wally. What have I got to do to get it into your thick heads that something is going on up at that field. Something that you…," stabbing Manning in the chest with his finger, "… should be investigating."

Ignoring Bill's finger, Manning calmly advised, "Go home, Bill. Go back to London and forget about that field."

Bill turned and stomped into the kitchen, slamming the door behind him. Leaning with his back to a counter he clenched his fists in utter frustration as he fumed at the conversation he had just had with Manning.

Why didn't Manning believe him? Why doesn't *anyone* believe him?

He didn't hear Manning and Mel talking in the cafe area, so he didn't hear them discussing his appearance and agreeing that Bill needed some help.

Chapter 29

Mel tried to calm Bill down after Manning had left the cafe, but to no avail. He was so hyped up with adrenalin that it would take several hours for Bill's blood pressure to return to normal. She decided to leave him to let off steam in his own way.

Without saying a word, Bill departed from the cafe and made straight for the rail station. He was going to have a few words with Wally about Manning, and he was going to make sure that Wally listened and, importantly, did something about the sergeant's attitude toward Bill.

By the time the train arrived in London Bill had calmed down. He was still angry about the way Manning had spoken to him, but his tongue lashing to Wally could wait. His first port of call was his office. In his haste to return to London he had left all the firm's checked reports back at the manor.

He was greeted firstly by the receptionist, then Julie. Deep in thought, he ignored them both. Julie picked up the phone to let Elle know that Bill had arrived.

As he sat at his desk, reflecting on the morning's train crash of events, Elle gently knocked on his door and peered inside. With a look of disbelief, she entered the room and stood facing Bill, shocked and trying to comprehend the sight in front of her. Bill had not shaved, or even washed, for days. His hair was matted and dishevelled, he was wearing the same clothes that he wore the last time he visited the office, and it was obvious that he had slept in them. His eyes darted from one place to another, as if he was searching for something that only he could see. He was a mess.

Constantly rubbing his face, he glared, open eyed, at Elle as she stood in the doorway to his office.

Elle spoke first. "Dad…," she said. No response.

"Dad!" she repeated, this time with some potency.

Bill eyes suddenly focused in recognition of his daughter.

"Hello, Elle. How's things?"

"I'm okay… But what's happened to you?" she asked, concerned about Bill's appearance.

"Me? I'm fine," volunteered Bill, unconvincingly, "why do you ask?"

"Look at you," exclaimed Elle, "you're a mess. What have you been doing to yourself?"

Looking down at his creased and unkept appearance Bill just smiled weakly and said, "Oh, I might have had a few drinks."

Behind Elle he saw Brad propping up the door frame.

"Come in, Brad. Come in. Let's have a party," sniggered Bill, waving his arms around the room in exasperation as if he was inviting the whole office into his domain.

Brad entered the room and sat opposite him.

"You're a bloody mess," he said.

Bill smiled an ingenuous smile. "Yeah, I know. Elle just told me."

Brad sat forward and, in earnest, asked Bill, "What the hell have you been doing? Look at the state you're in. Why haven't you cleaned yourself up?"

Bill just sat and stared firstly at Brad, then at Elle. Looking down and inspecting his scruffy appearance, Bill blew out a long lungful of stale breath and returned his eyes to Elle.

He placed his hands on the desk, palms down, and said, with a sardonic smile, "I've seen Amy…" His face took on a manic look, an ingenuous smile displaying un-brushed teeth, eyes wide open.

Brad and Elle stared at him with a mixture of puzzlement and disbelief. Neither of them spoke.

Bill repeated, "I've seen Amy. It's true. I spoke to her last night."

Elle was dumbstruck. Tears began to form in her eyes. Brad spoke up with a response that was bordering on the sympathetic.

"It's not possible, Bill. You know she's dead."

"I know that, but I'm telling you, I saw her last night… And I spoke to her." Bill's voice was now agitated and loud. Not even he believed what he was saying.

"What did you talk about?" asked Brad.

"Oh, nothing. She just told me that Elle was in danger, but everything's okay 'cos she says she will look after her."

"It's not possible, Bill…"

Brad's words were cut short by Elle. "Dad, why don't you come to my place for a while and get some rest. It doesn't look as if you've slept for days."

Brad interjected, "Bill, take some time off. Get some rest. You're not right, Bill. You're seeing things. Can't you see that?"

Hands upturned in a resigned posture, Bill said, "Yeah, I know, but nobody believes me. I've seen things on that field that nobody should witness," cried Bill with tears now in his eyes. "I've seen people beaten mercilessly, and I've seen people murdered and I've reported it to the police… But nobody believes me."

He cradled his head in his hands and sobbed. It was too much for Elle and she turned and left the room. Brad went round the desk to comfort Bill, placing an arm around his shoulder.

Downstairs, in the reception, Mel was asking to see Elle. She guessed that Bill may have returned to the office, but she didn't really know. She had decided to come talk to Elle, to let her know that Bill needed some help. She didn't know that Elle already knew that, but she was about to find out.

Seeing the firm's doctor enter the building, the receptionist interrupted Mel's question and stood to speak to the doctor.

"Brad's waiting for you upstairs, doctor." She buzzed the doctor through the turnstile, and he made his way to the lifts.

Mel looked back at the receptionist and questioned, "Doctor? You just called that man 'Doctor'?"

"Yes, Brad called him in to see Bill. I've not been up there, but I understand Bill's not well."

Mel didn't wait for permission, she headed for the lifts. Arriving at Bill's floor, the lift doors opened, and she was greeted by Elle who had been waiting for her. The receptionist had telephoned Elle to let her know that Mel was on her way up.

The two women hugged each other, and Elle brought Mel up to speed, finishing with, "… He's settled now that the doc' has given him a sedative, but he's not a pretty sight. Are you sure you want to see him?"

"Yes. I knew something was wrong when he came into the cafe earlier today."

Mel then brought Elle up to speed with the events that took place at the cafe earlier.

"Take me to him," Mel confirmed.

Bill was on a different cloud when Mel entered his room. In a haze he saw her and between sobs he said, "Nobody believes me."

"I know," sympathised Mel, "just rest for now and we'll sort it all out later."

In the depths of despair Bill repeated, in a confused and agitated state, "But nobody believes me."

The doctor moved forward. "He's in a very dark place right now. Let him rest for a while. The sedative I've given him should put him to sleep."

Everyone left the room, the women crying into their hankies and hanging on to each other's arms, Brad with his head down, stroking his chin in bewilderment. They all thought the same thoughts… That it was not like Bill to get into such a state as this.

They waited in reception as the ambulance arrived, and they watched as Bill was taken to hospital.

Chapter 30

Bill's recovery from a breakdown was, for him, long and hard.

The first few days were a haze of drugs to make him feel like he had had ten pints of beer before sending him back to sleep, and his memory of those days were, to say the least, foggy. Until he was taken off the sleep-inducing drugs, he had many recollections of the visions of Amy telling him that '...*Elle is in danger*', interspersed with visions of bully's twisted, distorted face. Whilst under the influence of the drugs he couldn't help thinking that bully's face was familiar, but he was unable to bring bully's true identity out of the mist.

In the weeks that he spent in hospital Bill had lots of rest, lots of counselling sessions and lots of visits from his friends and family.

Mel was invited to stay at the office flat while Bill recovered. She closed the cafe with a sign saying that she would '... be away for a while,' and she spent much of her time at Bill's bedside. She was relieved daily by Brad, Elle and Wally.

Eventually, Bill was well enough to leave hospital after promising to return at intervals to complete his counselling sessions. Elle offered to take him in, but Mel insisted that he stayed with her in the rooms above the cafe. She persuaded everyone that she could better keep her eye on him if he was close by her and having him in Colbert Village would ease Elle's burden of looking after Bill while trying to fit in with her busy work schedule. It was a plan that everyone accepted. Driving Bill's car, she took him to the cafe and made him comfortable before re-opening the tearoom.

The journey to Colbert Village was subdued as Bill looked out of the car window at the passing fields and trees, but Mel didn't press Bill to speak. His journey back to full health, she had been told by the hospital doctor, would be a long and patient one.

Inwardly, Bill's mind kept returning to Colbert's Field with its pristine manor and five picture postcard cottages. What was it about this field that nagged at his conscience? Why was this field calling to him to return? Why did it have such violent connotations? What did it want Bill to do? Something else that nagged at Bill was the fact that it was now twelve months since Amy's death, but Wally had not yet come up with anything to pinpoint the perpetrator.

All these questions needed answers, but Bill knew that he would not be able to fully recover until he had found the answers to those questions.

After a fortnight living at Mel's place, he began to feel bored and restless.

He occasionally helped Mel in the cafe, but most days he sat staring out of the bedroom window, or watching the TV, or sleeping. He thought to himself that it was, perhaps, time to snap out of his fog of self-pity, pull himself together and get on with life as he once knew it. Mel had been a rock to him during his 'dark times' but he accepted that she was not going to be as patient with him for ever. After dumping the remains of his medication in the bin he pulled on his coat and decided that it was time to confront the field… And all the demons that it accommodated. Bouncing down the stairs he was met at the bottom by Mel.

"Hello, lover. Are you going somewhere?" Mel was hesitant to let him go out alone, but she had a cafe full of tourists and could not leave.

"Yep, just out for a walk. I reckon some fresh air will do me good."

"Okay, but don't go too far."

Bill inwardly smiled as he compared himself to a young schoolboy going out to play.
He had made his mind up that the field had beckoned to him for long enough.

Closing the cafe door behind him, Bill stood looking at the sky and taking in the warm Autumn sunshine.

Once again, he met the old couple that had passed the time of day with him previously on the high street. He never knew where this couple were going. Never thought about it until now, but as he stepped forward the old man spoke up.

"Going for a walk?"

"Yeah. Thought I'd get some fresh air," answered Bill.

"That'll make you feel better," the old woman said with a kind smile. "You'll soon be back to your old self again."

"Maybe," said Bill. He was a little puzzled that they knew about his recent illness. Perhaps Mel had told them? Brushing the comment to one side, Bill asked, "Where are you two off to?"

"Nowhere in particular. Like you, we're just out enjoying the sun," the woman volunteered.

Before Bill could say another word, the old gentleman spoke up. "You haven't changed your mind about building houses on that field, have you?"

197

That question again.

"Nooo…," chuckled Bill, "I've not decided what to do with it yet, but you have my word that I'm not going to build any houses on it."

With an agreeing nod, the old chap smiled and said, "That's good. Next time you see the young policeman, say hello from us, will you?"

"Yes, of course," confirmed Bill.

"Let him know that we're always here if he needs us," the old woman said.

The old man joked, "And tell him that he can keep that fiver he took from my wallet that Saturday," grinning from ear to ear.

"I will do," confirmed Bill.

He was just about to ask their names when the cafe door opened.

Mel poked her head out and said to Bill, "Oh, it's you. I heard someone talking." Looking round, Mel asked, "Who were you talking to?"

Bill turned to face her. "Oh, just a nice old couple that I've met."

"You're not going back to the field are you, Bill?"

"I have to go back there to get my stuff," contended Bill.

"Please don't go," pleaded Mel, "You know it's not good for you."

"I'll be all right. Don't fuss, and don't worry."

"I just want you to be safe."

She gave him a loving kiss and looked in his eyes, hoping he would change his mind. Bill turned back to ask the old couple their names, but they were gone. Out of sight.

He made his way towards the manor, looking back occasionally to see Mel watching him from the cafe doorway.

Chapter 31

Iceberg Rose Cottage

Walking along the road, Bill reflected on recent events. His better nature told him that it was stupid to return to the field that had brought him so much trouble, especially as he was still recovering from a serious nervous breakdown. But the call of the field was too strong. Having said that, Bill now considered that the unfortunate episode, and subsequent enforced rest, had made him feel stronger within himself. Better able to face whatever the future brought. As he walked down the country lane, he clenched his fists and gritted his teeth, determined that no matter what happens from now on nothing like that will ever put him back in hospital.

On the way he happened upon George, Colbert Village's builder come handy man repairing a drystone wall.

"Morning, George," with a cheery smile.

"Mind how you go," was the response from George's default miserable face, without looking up. Bill walked on by, paying no heed to George's words of wisdom.

He felt edgy as he passed through the gate and walked up the hill towards the manor. Approaching the courtyard he looked round nervously, as if he was expecting something unexpected to happen. Walking towards the manor he routinely looked up at his bedroom window. No shadow ducking behind the curtain. He now felt slightly more at ease.

Out of interest, he turned and looked into Sunrise Rose Cottage. It was empty. Nothing in it to show that it had been occupied by anyone at all.

Inside the manor, he made a mug of coffee and made a cursory glance in each of the downstairs rooms to make sure everything was as he had left it. Entering the bedroom, he reclaimed his suitcase from a cupboard and started to fill it with clothes. He had been persuaded by Mel that the cafe should be his new permanent abode, a persuasion he readily agreed to. His frequent trip to the cupboards was interrupted when he heard people arguing outside. Out of curiosity he went over to the window.

Looking down he saw bully remonstrating with Charlotte. He quietly opened the window to listen in to what was being said.

"You're seeing somebody else, aren't you?" bully shouted.

"No, Robert. It's all in your mind," Charlotte shouted back.

With a swipe of his fist, he punched Charlotte in the face and hissed, "Lying bitch."

Charlotte fell back against her cottage door, trying to clear her head. Bully moved forward but stopped a short distance from her.

Charlotte wiped the blood from her mouth and retorted, "I saw what you did at Alaska Rose Cottage, Robert. I saw you torch it after you murdered that woman. Hit me one more time and I'll tell the police what I saw."

This enraged bully. "You won't. You'd better not!" he threatened.

"Why? What are you going to do about it? Run away again?"

Bully's face became distorted with rage. "I'll fucking kill you, you stupid cow," punching her in the stomach.

After coughing some blood away from her mouth, she brazenly goaded, "Yeah? Like you did that old woman in Gloriana? I bet it was you that drowned that girl."

Bully grabbed her by the throat and held her against the door. In defence, Charlotte grabbed a handful of his blonde hair and tried to push his head away from her face. Bully let go of her neck and twisted her wrist from the top of his head, roaring like an injured animal as she pulled a handful of hair from his scalp.

This was bully's cue to lay into Charlottes face with more punches. She fell to the ground, unconscious. Bill stood to dash downstairs but halted when he saw bully pick Charlotte up and carry her back into the cottage. Charlotte's hand drooped over bully's shoulder and Bill saw it clasping the locks of his blonde hair.

Bill raised his phone and took a couple of pictures of bully carrying Charlotte over the threshold to her cottage. He then stabbed Wally's number into it.

"Wally, you remember when I told you about that woman who was assaulted in one of these cottages?"

"Yeah. You haven't gone back to that field, have you?"

"Well, I've just seen him beat her up again. She looked to be in a bad way 'cos he had to carry her back into the cottage. I've just sent you a photo."

"Bill, you know what the doctor said about not going back to that field. Why have you gone and done exactly what he told you not to do? You don't want to finish up in there again, do you?"

"Wally! The woman needs help. I'm going over there to help her."

Before Wally could respond Bill cut him off and made his way downstairs. Exiting the manor, he saw bully close the cottage door behind him and make his way towards the bridge.

"Oi! You! What have you done to her?" shouted Bill.

Bully turned to face him, his face all sweaty and his teeth baring in anger.

"Nothing. Mind your own business!" he spat.

With that he turned and ran towards the bridge.

Bill wasn't satisfied with bully's answer, and he marched to Iceberg Rose Cottage. He found the door locked, so he rapped on it and shouted "Charlotte!"

No response.

"Charlotte, are you okay?"

Still no response

He kicked the door open. Inside he was brought to a sudden halt as he saw that the lower rooms were, unexpectedly, empty. Dashing upstairs to Charlotte's bedroom he found the same. All the rooms at first floor level were also empty. Nothing in any of them. No furniture, no curtains, no carpets and, disturbingly... No Charlotte!

Bill slowly walked downstairs, trying to make sense of what he had seen... Or not seen as the case may be. He looked into every one of the other cottages that stood unpretentiously before the manor. Everyone was empty. Even Alaska Rose Cottage, in its burnt-out, charred state looked tenacious, unapologetic for its demise.

Bill tried to phone Mel. White noise.

He tried to phone Wally. White noise.

He tried to phone Manning. Just more white noise.

'*This time,*' Bill thought, '*they have to believe me.*'

He took several pictures of the cottages and the manor.

Returning the phone to his pocket he slowly and thoughtfully made his way back to the cafe.

Sitting down at his usual table, Bill stared out of the window while Mel brewed a mug of coffee for him.

The old couple sauntered by and gave him a cheery wave. Bill waved back.

Mel had returned with his coffee, and she stood behind him, watching him wave through the window. She bent down to see who he was waving at, but it seemed that whoever it was had walked off.

"Enjoyed your walk?" she asked.

"Er, yeah," replied Bill, inattentively.

She sat down opposite him.

"You've been to that field, haven't you?"

"Guilty," replied Bill, a little embarrassed at being found out. He offered a contrite face to Mel that was clearly unaccepted.

Taking a deep breath, she looked back into his face and asked, "And what do you think you've seen this time?"

This annoyed Bill. He retorted, angrily, "I don't think it, Mel. I saw it!"

Mel could see that this conversation was in danger of getting out of hand. She placed her hand on top of his.

"It's all right, darling. Tell me what I can do to help you."

"You can't do anything. You don't believe me, nobody believes me, so I may as well just ignore what I saw."

"No, don't do that. What did you see?"

Bill described what he saw. Mel looked impassive while he related the events to her.

When he had finished, he looked down at the tablecloth and, in a subdued voice, said, "I'm losing it, again, aren't I?"

"I don't know, Bill... Tell you what, I'll let Wally know what you saw and see if he wants to take any action about it. Okay?"

Bill just returned a doleful nod of his head.

"What's the point, Mel? I doubt that he, or anyone, will do anything. I may as well just forget it happened."

Mel stood and took his mug of cold coffee back to the kitchen for a fresh refill. While she was there, she telephoned Wally.

She then put a chair out in the front garden and returned to persuade Bill to relax in the warm sunshine with today's newspaper. He surrendered to her wishes, half feeling sorry for himself and half not wanting to upset Mel any more than she already was.

The warm August sunshine made him a little sleepy and he dozed in the chair for a while. Just as Bill was entering a soothing dream state, he was brought back to the present abruptly with someone saying to him, "Hello, young man."

He rubbed his eyes open and peered into the bright sunlight. The old couple were stood at the gate smiling at him.

"It's a lovely day, isn't it?" the old man asked. "Did you give that young policeman my message?" smiling amiably.

"Er no, not yet. Sorry, haven't seen him lately but when I do, I'll tell him you asked after him."

"Yes, please do," the old woman said. "Mel's a lovely girl, isn't she?"

Bill smiled back with blushing cheeks. "Yes, she is," he replied.

"She will make a good wife for someone," the woman said, looking at her husband. They both laughed.

"Goodbye, for now," the man said, and they both turned and carried on walking down the street.

"Wait!" Bill shouted, "I forgot to ask your names."

The old couple either didn't hear him or they just ignored him as they turned into the path leading to the police station and disappeared behind the shops.

Bill returned to his siesta.

He woke with a start when Mel shook his shoulder.

"Wakey, wakey. It's lunch time."

She had erected a folding table in front of him and brought out another chair for herself.

"Feeling better?"

"Yeah, much," he answered.

They both enjoyed a salad lunch. Mel was careful not to broach any subject related to the field, although she was concerned that Bill had shown signs of a regression back to his illness.

Collecting up the lunch plates, she made her way back into the cafe. Bill heard the telephone inside the cafe ring. Mel answered it and had a small discussion with the caller before bringing the phone outside and handing it to Bill.

"It's Sergeant Manning," she said. "He just wants a quick word with you."

With his heart in his hands, Bill took the phone from Mel and put it to his ear.

"Hello?"

"Mr. Colbert... Bill, this is Sergeant Manning. How are you? I'm not disturbing you, am I?"

"No, not at all. I'm fine, thanks. What can I do for you?"

"I was wondering if you could come down to the station for a few minutes."

"I can, but why?"

"Oh, I thought I would give you an update on that assault you witnessed."

"Really? That was ages ago. I didn't think you would spend any time on it."

"You do me an injustice, Bill. Will you come in this afternoon?"

"I suppose so. I'll bring Mel with me, if it's okay."

"No problem, at all. Shall we say around one-thirty p.m.?"

"Okay."

Bill disconnected the call and returned the phone to the cafe. He thought to himself *'What's the point? Nothing's going to be done…,'* but there was no harm in having a walk in this bright sunshine. It might make him feel better.

Handing the phone to Mel, he said, "Manning wants me to go to the station this afternoon. Do you fancy a walk down there?"

"Sure," answered Mel. "I'll just wash up and then I'll be ready."

Bill returned the chairs and table back into the cafe and helped Mel with the washing up.

After brushing her hair, applying some lipstick and brushing down the front of her dress with her hands, they both ambled towards the station.

Chapter 32

At the station Manning lifted the counter flap to permit access to the inner sanctum for Bill and Mel.

On the way through the gap Bill nodded to the young constable. He was about to say to him that the old couple had sent their best wishes, when Manning interrupted his thoughts.

"Can you brew a few mugs of tea please, Peter? I'm sure Mr. Colbert will want one in due course."

"Yes, Sergeant," answered the PC and he turned and disappeared into the station kitchen, located behind the counter.

Bill and Mel followed Manning to Manning's office. Sat comfortably in an easy chair, Bill's eyes wandered around, surveying its contents. The shelves were cluttered with an assortment of books and manuals, interspersed with ornaments. Manning's hat hung on the back of the door. His desk faced the window so as to capture the light shining from the outside, but Manning rotated his chair to face his guests and he sat with half a dozen files laid out on a coffee table in between them.

Turning to Mel he asked, "Have you told him about Charlotte, yet?"

On hearing Charlotte's name Bill suddenly became interested in the meeting.

"What Charlotte?" he shot at Manning.

Mel answered Manning's question. "No, not yet. I was waiting for an opportune moment."

Looking from Mel to Manning Bill repeated, "What Charlotte?"

"Manning spoke calmly. "You reckon now is about the best time?"

Bill's patience was being stretched to its limit. "What Charlotte?" he demanded forcefully.

Mel turned to face Bill and put his hands in hers. Sucking in a deep breath, she exhaled half of it and related Charlotte's history to Bill.

"You remember that I told you that I once had a sister, and that she had died in her twenties?"

"Yes, when we first met." Bill had calmed down and sat in anticipation of what Mel was about to say.

"Well Charlotte… The Charlotte that lived in Iceberg Rose Cottage… Was that sister."

She waited while Bill absorbed the information.

One word came out of Bill's mouth. "Lived?"

"Yes. I wanted to tell you so many times, but Sergeant Manning asked me not to while he conducted his enquiries. Can you ever forgive me?" Tears filled her eyes and rolled down her cheeks. Bill ignored them and stared daggers at Manning.

"Why? Why did you ask her not to say anything?" Bill shouted, angrily, at Manning.

"Because I didn't want you getting involve and prejudicing my enquiries," Manning offered up.

"What do you mean? What enquiries?"

"Tell him the rest," prompted Manning to Mel.

Bill turned to face Mel once more.

She continued, "At the time, everyone thought she had committed suicide. I found her hanging from a beam in her bedroom one morning in 2001…"

Bill interrupted her. "What? You couldn't have. I just saw her, this morning!"

"It's true, Bill. Robert Mathews wheedled his way into Iceberg in 2000 and was living with Charlotte," Mel said. "He constantly ill-treated her. Had done from the time they first met. He was a bad man... An evil man. She wanted to leave him and tried to several times, but he always found her and brought her back. The field was his domain. A territory that he controlled. Everyone in those cottages despised him, but they were all also frightened of him."

Out of her handbag she produced an envelope and opened it to give Bill its contents. Bill saw that it was Charlotte's death certificate. He studied the typing, homing in on the date and time of death. There it was... ten-twenty a.m. on the twentieth day of August 2001. In disbelief, Bill looked at Mel and Manning, in turn, then returned his gaze to the death certificate. She had, indeed, been found by Melissa Wright, Charlotte's sister, that morning. The address confirmed what Mel had just disclosed; *Iceberg Rose Cottage, Colbert's Field, Colbert Village Essex.* The cause of death was shown as *Death by asphyxiation as a direct result of hanging.*

Manning took over the reins from Mel. "Do you want me to continue?"

Staring at the death certificate, Bill just nodded his head. A slight, almost imperceptible nod.

Manning opened one of the files to begin his lengthy narrative. On the top page was a picture of a young boy, about eight or nine years of age. Bill immediately recognised the face looking at him from the file. It was Ezra.

"First, I should give you a bit of background into the field. What's gone on over the years. Are you happy with that?" Manning asked.

Another slight nod from Bill, now concentrating his gaze on Manning. Mel budged up closer to Bill and hooked onto his arm, presumably, Bill thought, for comfort and support. He welcomed the move and smiled at Mel.

The young PC brought in a tray with the mugs balanced on top, a packet of biscuits under his arm. Placing these on the table in front of them, he departed and closed the door behind him.

Manning took a sip of tea, sat back and started his speech.

"Them there cottages on Colbert's Field are as old as the manor," he said. "They were all built, with the manor, by the farmer that owned the land. A bloke called Willum Colbert; I think."

Bill Interjected, "Yes, he was my ancestor. I inherited the field from him."

"Okay," continued the Sergeant. "When you first came to the station with an allegation of Charlotte's assault, I telephone a friend of mine for some information. I wanted to know more about Charlotte… Where she lived, whether she was married, that sort of thing.

"The guy I spoke to, was the previous Sergeant in charge of this station. Sergeant Michael Needham. He told me that there was a file in central archives in London, and that I should go look-see what it had to say. He also told me that Charlotte had appeared to have committed suicide, but that there were questions surrounding her death. I went down to the Met's archives in London and extracted all these files." Manning patted the pile of files in front of him.

While Manning was speaking Bill's eyes had homed in on a photo on his desk… A photo of a homely old couple, arm-in-arm and smiling back at the camera.

As soon as Manning paused for a breath Bill asked, "Who's that couple in the photo on your desk?"

"Oh, they're my parents. Why?"

"I spoke to them this morning."

Manning's eyes almost popped out of their sockets.

"Can't have done, Bill. They died in 2003 when I was just nineteen years old."

Bill smiled at Manning, and then burst out laughing.

"What? What's so funny?" Manning asked.

"Your mum sends her love, and your dad says you can keep that fiver you took from his wallet that Saturday night."

Manning's hand shook, spilling soe tea on his trousers. "How did you know about that?" he questioned.

"He told me," Bill answered, calmly.

Manning sat back in his chair and stared at Bill for, perhaps, thirty seconds. With a jolt he broke the silence that had descended upon the room, pulled himself together, picked up the telephone and stabbed a key.

"More tea!" he ordered, all the while staring at Bill.

After a brief pause, he looked back into the file on his lap and continued his dialogue.

"Anyway, Ezra Hugo Kendrick was born on the first of April 1967. April Fool's Day. His parents considered this date to be a bad omen for the birth of their son and from the moment Mrs. Kendrick left hospital and brought him back to Pilgrim Rose Cottage they both abused young Ezra relentlessly. They were reported to Social Services regularly for neglecting him, but for whatever reason Social Services didn't consider it necessary to remove him from his parent's constant abuse. His early life was one of regular beatings by them both and he was starved of both love and, indeed, food. He was frequently found rummaging in his neighbour's bins for scraps. Not a happy childhood.

"On the evening of his birthday on the first of April 1975, when he was just eight years old, Ezra snapped and murdered his parents. All this happened at Pilgrim Rose Cottage. Tell me something, Bill. You say you saw this happen. What did Ezra use to murder his parents?"

"He slammed an axe into his dad's head while he slept and then stuck a knife into his mother's neck."

"Did you see what kind of knife? A kitchen knife? A pen knife? A table knife?"

"None of those. It was a hunting knife. It had a thick bone handle and a pointed blade with a serrated edge. I wrote this down in my statement… Which you took."

"But these details were never released to the public, Bill. How did you come to have them?"

"I saw it happen!" He turned to Mel. "I saw it happen Mel. Tell me you believe me."

Manning jumped in. "It's okay, Bill. We believe you. We all believe you," calming Bill's agitated state. "Have a drink of tea and I'll tell you what happened next."

Bill slurped a mouthful of tea and put the mug back on the tray.

Manning continued. "I honestly don't know how you know this but let me continue."

Another imperceptible nod from Bill.

"Ezra was taken into custody…"

Bill interrupted. "I watched it happen."

"Yes, it's in your statement. Anyway, Ezra was taken into custody and after he had been assessed by Social Services, a doctor *and* a child psychiatrist he was sectioned and put into a mental health institution. He was in there for ten years. During that period, he hardly spoke, he never played with any toys, and he was in what appeared to be self-inflicted solitary confinement. He didn't have any education to speak of. He was given the opportunity to mingle with the other patients, but he never took it.

"In 1985 he was re-assessed for the hundredth time, and he was deemed fit enough to be released. The hospital authorities didn't consider him a risk to society because he had accepted his fate inside the institute and had never caused or been involved in any trouble in any way whatsoever. They considered him to be a quiet lad, harmless to anyone and everyone. It is believed that he went back to his home in Pilgrim Rose Cottage. Do you want to take a break?"

"No, thanks. I'm fine. Keep going."

"The same year he was released from the hospital, 1985, an elderly lady was murdered in Gloriana Rose Cottage. She was kicked to death."

Bill looked up. "I told you that, as well."

"Yes, you did. What else can you tell me about that incident?"

"I wrote it all down. It's on file."

Manning closed the file on his lap and opened the next one in the pile. Deliberately placing the file in front of him, Manning asked him to take a look at the crime scene photo.

"That's her. That's the old woman. Look her cat is still sitting in her rocking chair."

"Yes, it's Mrs. Brownlow. What else do you know? How did she finish up on the floor?"

"I saw a youth loitering in the hallway. The old woman opened her lounge door and they both went to stand next to the fireplace. I've told you this. I've written it down for you."

"Yes, but keep going."

"She took a bowl from the mantlepiece and gave the youth a wad of notes that was inside it."

"Carry on."

"The youth smashed the bowl over her head, and she went down like a ton of bricks. The youth then kicked her in the face. He left the cottage. I chased after him, but he got away."

"Can you tell me what kind of bowl, was it?"

"It was a rare piece. A rare Wedgwood Fairyland Lustre 'Geisha/Angels' patterned octagonal bowl if I remember correctly. Worth about £2400 in today's terms. Why?"

"You're right. It was a rare Wedgwood Fairyland Lustre 'Geisha/Angels' patterned octagonal bowl," replied Manning as he read from the file. "A forensic lab pieced together the shards of the broken pottery and they had it verified by an antique specialist. I needn't have asked you, knowing what you do for a living, but this information was never made public. So how do you know what it was?"

"I told you. I saw it on the mantlepiece before she took it down."

Manning took another long look at Bill and returned to his files. Closing the one on his lap he substituted it with the next one in the pile.

"Do you want a break?" he asked.

Bill just looked into his face.

"Let's look at Sunrise Rose Cottage, shall we?" opening this file.

Bill hesitantly asked Manning, "Do I need a lawyer?"

He felt Mel flinch and he looked up to see Manning staring intently at him.

"What do you think, Bill. Do you need a lawyer?"

"I... I... No, I don't think I need a lawyer. I've done nothing wrong. Am I under arrest?"

Mel flinched again.

"No, you're not under arrest, Bill. Are you sure you don't want to take a break? You're looking quite tired."

"No, I don't want to take a break. What about Sunrise Rose Cottage?"

"One year after the woman was found dead in Gloriana by her daughter, a young, eighteen-year-old Janine Potter was found face down in the trout stream."

Bill sat in silence, waiting for Manning to continue.

"She was visiting her grandparents in Sunrise Rose Cottage at the time. She had been stripped, raped and throttled. According to the postmortem, she died at around ten p.m. on a June evening. Her grandparents told the police that she went out at about that time for a stroll down the riverbank. Do you know anything about that incident, Bill?"

Bill searched his memory, but nothing came to mind.

"Let's take a break," he said.

Everyone stood and stretched. They all went outside for some fresh air while the young PC put the kettle on, once more.

As they stood outside the station, idly chatting about nothing in particular, Manning took Bill to one side and whispered, "Thanks for telling me what Dad said. I must admit that I've been feeling guilty about nicking that fiver ever since I nicked it," he joked.

"Let it go, Sergeant. I'm sure they will have forgiven you before now."

"Yeah, maybe so," replied Manning, in agreement.

After a short break they all returned to Manning's office.

"Now, where were we?" he asked, more to himself than anyone else. "Oh, yes. Sunrise Rose Cottage. Have you had any more thoughts about it?"

"Yes," answered Bill, "I recollect seeing a youth follow her down to the bridge. He was hiding in the bushes next to Sunrise when she came out."

Bill was now feeling more confident that he was being believed about his sightings and he talked freely and without hesitation.

Manning prompted him some more. "Can you recall what she was wearing?"

"Yes. I first saw her when I returned to the manor after a bit of fishing in the river. It was late afternoon, and she was gardening in front of Sunrise. She had on a gold top that shimmered in the sunlight. She was also wearing green, ankle length wellies and a dress with a summer pattern on it - flowers and things.

"Much later, I suppose around eight or nine o'clock, I was on my way to bed, and I saw her leave Sunrise. She spoke to someone in the cottage then made her way towards the bridge. I saw the youth follow her and I dashed downstairs to follow him. I had to put my trousers back on, so by the time I'd dashed downstairs he was in the distance. I didn't see the young lady, but when I got close to the bridge, I heard her scream."

"What did you do then?"

"I thought the scream came from the other side of the river, so I dashed across the bridge and tried to see where the youth had gone. After about an hour I couldn't find either of them, so I went back to the manor. I thought about informing you, but with nothing to find I honestly didn't think you would believe me. I had it in the back of my mind that *if* anything had happened to her the folks in the cottage would report it soon enough. Anyway, if you remember you didn't exactly treat me as if you believed what I had reported to you previously."

"You're right about that, and I apologise for not taking you seriously enough. Again, the clothes she wore were never made public, and the grandparents, according to the file, promised not to say a word.

"That was in 1986 and we suspect that Ezra was guilty of both those murders; in Gloriana and at Sunrise, but there was never enough forensic evidence to tie him to either of the crimes. He was interrogated quite extensively about the murders, even with a forensic psychologist present during every minute of his questioning, but we had to release him. After the Sunrise incident he disappeared without trace. He didn't reappear until 1999."

Manning picked up the remaining file from the coffee table.

"The next record we have of his existence is when neighbours reported to Mel that Charlotte had been slapped around in the garden of Iceberg Rose Cottage. Mel approached us, but because we considered it as a domestic squabble we didn't want to get involved and we let the file lie dormant for a while.

"He had surfaced under the name of Robert Mathews. That's where you come into this. In January 2023, you came to the station to report an assault. Remember?"

"Yes. You told me you would look into it, but I wasn't all that convinced you would."

"When you reported that Charlotte had been abused I couldn't, at that time, believe your story. Charlotte had been dead for twenty-two years. How could I believe you. It was accepted around these parts that she had committed suicide in 2001. Even Mel accepted it, so how could *anyone* believe that you had seen her being abused?

"I kept quiet to protect you, Bill. If I had made any formal record, we would have had a whole army of men in white coats come down here to cart you off."

Bill spoke back to Manning in defiance. "That's exactly what happened, Manning. Nobody believed me. After what you've just told me I'm finding it difficult to believe it myself. But I saw these things. I saw what happened."

Manning stood and put a hand on Bill's shoulder to calm him down and keep him seated.

"We know, Bill. We know," he stressed. "We believe you."

Bill looked at Manning with more than a look of relief and with the tears of his frustration releasing him from his memory of the time he spent in hospital.

Manning sat back down.

"We're nearly finished Bill. Shall we carry on?"

Another imperceptible nod from Bill.

"Tell me what happened at Alaska Rose Cottage. Who torched it?"

"The same guy that beat Charlotte."

"Would you recognise him if you saw him again?"

"Most certainly." Bill's memory flashed back to the time bully had faced him and he thought he recognised something in bully's features.

"What happened?" asked Manning.

Bill continued. "Charlotte had given me the heads up on '*happenings*' at Alaska. At first, I didn't put much credence on her comments, but when I saw the guy creep across the courtyard and get invited into Alaska, I knew something was going on. Later on, I heard some bloke arguing with the guy outside Alaska. I can only assume that the second guy had returned unexpectantly and found something amiss in the cottage. I watched as the bully and this guy had a fight, and bully came off best. With the guy on the floor bully kicked him in the head. I went down to see if there was anything I could do, but the guy was dead. Bully disappeared into Iceberg.

"I dialled 999 but I got no signal, so I dashed down here to the station, but it was locked up for the night. I dialled Wally's number and got through to him. He told me he'd get in touch with you, so I returned to see what I could do for the woman who lived in Alaska. By the time I arrived the cottage was in flames. Wally had told me to wait at the cafe, so I went back there. That's when you came in to warn me off."

Manning looked a bit embarrassed. "Yeah, I remember. That fire took place in 2000, but again, with no evidence to point to Ezra we had to leave it on file as yet another open case, like we did with Gloriana and Sunrise. So how did you get involved with things that happened at Iceberg, in 2001?"

"When I reported the first assault to you, I didn't know about any of what you've just told me. As far as this assault is concerned, all I know is that bully beat her up in the garden and then carried her, unconscious into the cottage. I knew nothing about Charlotte's supposed suicide until Mel told me just now. I did hear a bit of the conversation before Charlotte was knocked out."

"Oh? Tell me more," prompted Manning.

"I heard Charlotte say that she saw what he did at Alaska and that if he didn't stop slapping her, she would report it to you guys. He beat her unconscious and carried her into the cottage."

Manning revived his dialogue. "From what we can ascertain, Robert Mathews strangled her then strung her up to make it look like it was suicide."

Mel sobbed into her hands. Bill held her closer to him in sympathy.

"How do you know it was Mathews?" he asked.

"Charlotte held on to a load of hair that she had pulled from his scalp. We got his identity from forensic records dating back to 1975, when Ezra killed his parents. The person you and Mel know as Robert Mathews is, in fact, Ezra Hugo Kendrick. He went on the run at the time Charlotte was murdered and he's been on the run since."

"Why can't you pick him up?" asked Mel.

"Because we can't find him, but when we do, he'll spend the rest of his life behind bars. I'm sorry they stopped hanging criminals in 1964. If I had my way, I'd be at the front of the queue to tie the knot around this bloke's neck."

Bill took out his phone. "I've got some photos of him if it helps."

"Those would be a great help in identifying him when he's caught. I'll put them on file. Let's have a look."

Bill opened his phone, homed in on his photo gallery and sat up straight, staring at the screen. The images in front of him showed nothing but a blank field. Bully wasn't there, the cottages weren't there. Just an empty field all the way down to the Trout stream. Bill shook his head.

"I definitely took some photos of him, and the cottages!" he declared with a puzzled look on his face.

"Not to worry," said Manning, "we've got enough with your statements and descriptions to put him away for good."

Manning wrapped up his history of the field. "After Charlotte was found by you, Mel, the local council decided to demolish all the cottages in 2016, similar to what happened to Fred West's house. They decided that there was too much bad history attached to that field and old George's firm was paid a princely sum to pull them down and landscape the field."

Bill looked at Mel with a furrowed brow then back at his phone, although he said nothing.

Manning turned to Bill. "Do you believe in ghosts, Bill?" he asked.

"I don't know what to believe," replied Bill. "All I know is what I saw."

"Well, I've never believed in them... Until now. Even now, I'm not sure what to believe, but you saw things that only the police knew of. Things that happened in the past. Things that could not have happened today, but I have to believe that you saw them."

"Thank you, Sergeant. So, you believe me now?"

"I do, indeed."

"So, what happens now?"

"Leave it with me, sir. We're looking into it, and we'll let you know." Manning was smiling a cheeky smile, the first time that Bill had seen him smile.

He and Mel returned to the cafe for a well-deserved meal… And the first good night's sleep in a long time for Bill.

Chapter 33

After Sergeant Manning's revelation of the field's history Bill decided to return to the manor to retrieve his belongings.

At the back of his mind were several questions; should he sell the field? If he did it was highly likely that some property developer would build a load of dreary, faceless houses that nobody in Colbert Village wanted. Mel would be none too pleased either. Should he continue to live in the manor? As attractive as that seemed it was doubtful that Mel, or anyone else would join him. What about converting the manor to an office and transferring everyone from London to work there. That would be expensive with refurbishment, relocation of staff, re-design of letterheads, etc., and there would probably be hiring of new staff in place of those that didn't want to relocate. Bill doubted that there would be much new blood in Colbert Village, so there would be advertising fees for new staff. And don't forget the mandatory office warming party for staff and clients. All-in-all, an expensive project that would need lots of management meetings and careful handling. Bill put the ideas on the back burner for a while. at least until he was in a position to concentrate better on them.

He also wanted to take some more photos of the place. The last ones he took didn't turn out too well. He asked Mel if she wanted to accompany him and she greed, reluctantly. Her own memories of the field, Charlotte in particular, were not ones that she wished to resurrect.

As the car bounced through the gates and up the hill towards the courtyard the butterflies in Mel's stomach told her that this was not, perhaps, the most desirable thing to do. After all, the field, and the manor, and the cottages were all part of Bill's catastrophic breakdown, and she didn't want him regressing back to that state.

She had no need to worry.

Bill brought the car to a sudden halt about thirty yards from the courtyard and got out of it. Standing there, his elbow on the car's roof, he stared at the field in total surprise. With his mouth open, his brow furrowed and a look of puzzlement on his face he muttered to himself, "What the...!"

Mel joined him and hooked her arm through his. "What's wrong?" she asked.

Bill stared at the field for a good forty seconds, his head turning and his eyes darting from one place to another. He looked at Mel in disbelief.

"They're gone!" he stated. "The cottages are gone!"

He looked at Mel. "They're all gone!" he repeated and then burst into a fit of laughter.

Mell looked puzzled.

"You know that." she said. "Manning told you that yesterday. They were demolished in 2016."

All that could be seen was an empty field with an abandoned, dilapidated manor. He drove to the courtyard and stood looking at the manor.

All that was left of the manor were broken windows and an open door that hung off one hinge. Not the pristine place he had seen when he first went to the field. It was a desolate, unwanted building with weeds growing inside and out, debris and broken glass littering the place.

They both went through the broken door, looking round at what years of abandonment had done to the place. The lounge that had once boasted fine furniture was empty except for the dust of ages and moth-eaten curtains almost hanging from the curtain rods. At the rear, where the kitchen was, stood, a lone rusting Aga, waiting for the fire that would never again be lit in its grate, next to it the rusty tin bath that Bill stood in to bathe after heating water on the Aga.

"Shall we get your stuff?" Mel asked, waking Bill from thoughts.

Bill looked around the room and wondered if he really had seen ghosts, or whether he had just imagined it all. Did he imagine Charlotte being abused? Did he imagine her undressing in her bedroom window? Did he imagine the murders? Did he follow the youth going to murder young Janine Potter, or Mrs. Brownlow with the valuable rare Wedgwood bowl?

He looked back at Mel.

"Did I imagine all that?" he asked.

"I don't know, Bill. Did you? If you imagined it all, how could you have known all those things you told Sergeant Manning about? All that information that was never released by the police?"

Bill shook his head. "Let's get my stuff."

They ascended the once grand staircase, now just a lonely stairway without the plush carpet that it once boasted.

Entering the master bedroom, Mel asked, "Did you really sleep in this place?"

Looking round, Bill let out a long breath of air. In the place where a four-poster bed would have been there was now just his sheets and blankets, laid out on the floor as if sitting on a mattress. Against the wall of the bedroom was a pile of his clothes, laid out in a row as if they had been hung up in a cupboard.

"Seems so," Bill replied with a smile.

At the foot of his 'bed' there was a lone chair facing the window with a naval telescope sitting on it.

"That's where I sat to witness what happened in the cottages," Bill said.

They both looked at each other, shrugged their shoulders and laughed. With a slight nod of his head, Bill considered his brush with ghosts to be at an end.

He would soon find out that he was wrong...

Bundling his belongings into a couple of bags he had brought, Bill vowed to find out more about his inheritance, and more about the people who lived on Colbert's Field.

PART 2

CAPTURE

Chapter 34

Bill and Mel returned to the cafe, chatting on the way.

"What are you going to do now?" asked Mel.

"First thing in the morning I'll nip into work, then I think I'll do a bit of research."

"Do you want any help with that?"

"Nah. I'll spend some time on the Internet before I come back here. Can you see if I'll be able to call into Colbert Observer's Office?"

"Yep. I'll let you know what time."

The following morning Bill finished his breakfast and made ready to catch the train to London. Mel took him to the station. After receiving a peck on the cheek, he boarded the train and found an empty seat. Travelling to London he had lots to think about.

Mel and the sergeant were right. How *did* he see all those goings on at the field when they happened in the past... And how was he able to interact with those people? He persuaded himself that he did witness those things and that he did, indeed, interact with Charlotte, the young boy, and Mrs. Brownlow and, not least, the bully. He wished he could meet that bully to show him precisely what pain feels like, but he didn't consider that old adage '...you need to be careful what you wish for.'

Arriving at the office he was welcomed by Elle and Julie. Sitting in Elle's office he explained to them his visit to Colbert police station, and the discussion that took place, followed by his trip back to the field with Mel and what he saw or, more precisely, what he *didn't* see! He was then given the third degree he was expecting whilst sat on the train. The usual questions around the what, why, how and when were thrown at him as he related his experiences to his audience, and everyone listened with open mouths. Brad had joined them halfway through the light-hearted interrogation.

Although there were many unanswered questions - questions that Bill just could not answer - they all appeared to be reasonably satisfied with Bill's responses.

Brad asked, "So what now, Bill? You ready for some proper work?"

Bill paused for thought, then answered, "I've given a lot of thought to my role here over the past few weeks and I've come to a result that I want you to consider."

Elle sat forward in silence, eyeing Bill suspiciously. "Oh? And what would that be?" she asked.

Bill continued. "I think we all accept that Mel and I are very much in love. Throughout all this she has been my rock, my listening post." Everyone nodded in agreement. "Well, what I really want to do is live with her permanently."

This produced a myriad of questions, all at once. Bill raised his hand to silence everyone.

"Firstly, I've got to ask her to marry me."

"You haven't asked her yet?" jumped in Elle. "Come on, Dad, you really do need to get a move on … It's getting too late for me to have a little brother!" Laughter bounced off the walls. Bill blushed and smiled.

"*If* she says yes then we have to sit down and talk about our futures. Now, what I would like *somebody* to do…," looking at Elle and Brad, "is to buy out my share of the partnership."

This, again, produced a multitude of questions, all at once. Again, Bill raised his hands to quieten down the throng.

"The way I see it is that you have all managed without me since I went into hospital back in July. That's almost two months ago …"

Brad decided to interrupt. "Yes, but that was out of necessity. We had to tick things over until you returned, and we've been running in emergency mode all this time."

"I take on board everything you say, Brad, and I really do appreciate all your patience while I've been 'doing my own thing'," two fingers dipped in the air to show Bill's meaning, "but just let me finish, and you'll all have a better picture." declared Bill.

"I'm not going to ask for so much that it will break the bank. My pension, when I can draw on it, will be sufficient to keep me in booze for me and chocolates for Mel so the pay-off for my half of the partnership will be peanuts, in comparison. But you will be one man down, so to speak, so…," another pause for thought and a look into Brad's face, "as a concession for my generosity I ask that Elle is made up to full partner status. She has worked for us for long enough, she knows the ropes, she is good with the clients, and I think she is up to it. What do you think, Brad?"

Brad looked from Bill to Elle and back. "Err … I … have never thought about it, but now you mention it I think you might have a point. What do you think, Elle?"

"But Dad …" This time, Bill interrupted.

"Elle, this is your time. It's your chance to be something. Be someone. I'm not doing this for you, I'm doing it for me. I need a fresh start. A new beginning, and I know that that beginning is with Mel, and, you never know, you might even get a baby brother."

With tears in her eyes Elle hugged Bill, then turned to Brad. Wiping her cheeks on a tissue that Julie had produced from nowhere, Elle confirmed to Brad that she would accept his offer, if it was made.

"Consider it done," said Brad.

Bill then continued, "Making Elle a partner gives you the opportunity to bring in some fresh blood. I suggest another Marketing Director to replace Elle and you should also hire another gofer to help out with the other stuff."

Brad laughed in response, "Two minutes out of the firm and he's already telling us what to do!" They all joined Brad's merriment. Then Elle asked, "Can I have Julie as my assistant?"

Brad and Bill looked at each other, they both held out a hand, palm down, and oscillated their hands ninety degrees, in uncertainty. They all finished the meeting in good spirits, laughing and joking until lunch time. Bill explained that, subject to Mel's agreement, he would become part of the cafe staff. An unpaid waiter and table-wiper.

Brad and Julie left Bill and Elle to chat in private.

"We'll be sorry to see you go, Dad. You've done so much with this firm, and I'm sure our long-standing clients will have something to say about it." Tears welled up in her eyes.

"It's not as if I'm going to live in a different country. Colbert Village is just half an hour on the train. Perhaps an hour at most by car."

"I know, but it won't sink in until tomorrow, when I realise that you won't be coming back into work."

"You'll survive. And think of the fun of moving into my office, with its view and extra cupboard storage for all those four-hundred-pound dresses that you can now afford to wear."

Elle slapped his arm in reprimand. They hugged each other for a long time, Bill's jacket soaking up the silent tears falling on his shoulder.

After a while Elle straightened up, wiped her face with Bill's pocket handkerchief and asked, "What now?"

"I'm going to do some research on the Internet, then I'm going to see what Mel says about having a partner at the cafe."

"She'd better say yes," demanded Elle.

They both departed to their own offices, Elle still wiping tears from her eyes and Bill deep in thought.

Chapter 35

Bill sat at his desk and typed out a formal resignation, with his suggestion for a pay-out from the firm. He pitched the pay-out deliberately low so as to show willing and to reinforce his request for Elle to be a full partner. Emailing this to Brad he then opened up his Internet search engine to begin his search of Colbert's Field and its occupants.

Surprisingly, the Internet didn't give him very much to go on. Colbert Village came up as a through route to the rest of Essex and there was a bit about the village itself; where it got its name, population, points of interest, etc. So, Bill went for newspaper information.

Calling up a newspaper archive website, he found several publications that pointed to articles related to the field.

The oldest article he found was in the Essex Newscast newspaper. This told the story of young Ezra Hugo Kendrick murdering his parents. This brought back Bill's memory of the event and he downloaded a copy of the article.

Boy murders his parents

Michael Prentiss

An 8 year old boy has murdered both his parents and has been taken into custody. Ezra Hugo Kendrick was found yesterday by police, naked and covered in blood, at his parent's home in Colbert Village, Essex.

The body of his father, John Kendrick, was found in his bed. He had been killed by a blow to the head. Ezra's mother, Mabel, was found lying on the floor of the lounge. No further information about the murders has been released by the police.

Ezra will be assessed by Social Services later today, but it is envisaged that he will probably be taken to a secure location while enquiries by the police are being conducted.

8 year old Ezra Hugo Kendrick

Referring to the notes that Mel took during Sergeant Manning's narrative on the history of the field Bill's next focus was on the murder of Susan Brownlow in Gloriana Rose Cottage. After several frustrating non-productive searches, he eventually found a reference to the Colbert Village Observer, although his search result didn't tell him much more.

'That's convenient,' thought Bill. *'Right on my doorstep.'*

He picked up his phone and dialled Mel. "Hiya, Mel. Have you been able to get in touch with the Observer? I've just found a reference to it about Susan Brownlow's murder, and I think I can get better details from them direct."

"Yes, this morning. They're open nine to three-thirty most weekdays, and you don't need an appointment to call in. Speak to a Joanna Smallbrook, the Editor."

"Magic! I'll call in tomorrow morning."

"Are you coming home yet?"

"Soon. I've just got a couple more things to look up then I'll be on my way."

Terminating the call, Bill made a note of the Observer's contact and returned to his laptop.

From Mel's notes he searched for Janine Potter. He found two references; one for Colbert's Observer, the other for The National News Reporter, dated twenty-fourth of June 1986. Ignoring the Observer's reference - he could look at this tomorrow - he called up the article from the National News Reporter

MISSING WOMAN FOUND MURDERED

Ben Havers

A young woman reported missing, from Colbert's Field, Colbert's Village, Essex, has been found murdered. She had not been seen since 9:00pm on the 22nd of June.

Janine Potter, 18, was visiting her grandparents at Sunrise Rose Cottage when she disappeared without trace. A search party was formed by the local police and a television appeal was held last night. Her parents arrived at Colbert Village police station, yesterday, and joined the search party. Her body was found, face down, in a nearby river. We understand that she had been stripped and raped before being drowned.

As soon as the body was discovered yesterday Inspector Les Prichard of Essex Police made the following statement:

"At approximately 7:15pm today, Monday the 23rd of June, the body of 18 year old Janine Potter was found in the river adjacent to Colbert's Field. She had been brutally raped before being drowned.

"Our thoughts and prayers go out to Janine's family and friends and a service will be held tomorrow evening at Colbert Village Chapel. Janine's family have asked that only close relatives and friends attend this service, and they ask that their privacy is respected at this particularly stressful time.

"Following the discovery, police forensics have worked tirelessly to collate evidence from the crime scene. The evidence, so far, suggests that a known criminal may well have been involved with this heinous crime and we are now searching for one of the occupants of Colbert's Field who, we believe, has fled the scene and gone to ground. His name is Ezra Hugo Kendrick. Kendrick is 19 years old, five feet eleven inches tall with blonde hair and was last seen wearing a dark anorak over blue jeans. I cannot stress enough that this man is extremely dangerous and should not be approached. If anyone knows the present location of this man they should contact us immediately. Kendrick is now considered to be a fugitive from the police and all sea and air ports and rail stations have been informed.

Ezra Hugo Kendrick

" Our investigations, so far, also revealed that he is suspected of another murder that took place at Colbert's Field last year. During that incident, an 85 year old woman was beaten to death.

We are appealing to anyone with information about either of these crimes to come forward. Sergeant Needham can be contacted at any time, day or night, at Colbert Village police station. It is imperative that we catch and detain this man as we suspect that he will kill again."

Janine's mother paid tribute to their "Beautiful, beautiful daughter." In a statement to reporters Mrs. Potter said: "[She] was loved by everyone that met her - not just Colbert Village, but everywhere she went... her vibrant and joyful life has been cut short and we are trying to come to terms with the fact that our loving daughter is no longer with us. Our lives will never be the same now that she has gone."

Janine's father then made his statement : "We appeal to whoever has done this to come forward and give yourself up. It is clear that you need help and we are confident that the authorities will treat you fairly and provide the help that I feel you need. Please give yourself up."

Police investigations continue.

The picture of Ezra jumped out at him. This was definitely the youth that he saw murder Susan Brownlow. Making a note to let Wally and Manning know, he also noted to review this article at the Observer tomorrow.

Turning his attention to the fire at Alaska Rose Cottage he once more found a reference to the Observer. He wrote another note to chase this one up tomorrow.

Finally, he searched for information on Charlotte's death and came up with an article in The British Independent Daily Journal, another national newspaper, this one distributed throughout the south of England. On calling up this particular article he sat back in utter surprise, totally gobstruck.

The British Independent Daily Journal - Monday, 3rd September, 2001

WOMAN FOUND HANGING IN HER BEDROOM

Is there a serial killer in Colbert Village?

Investigation by Jonathon Blaine

Last Friday afternoon, 31st. August, Charlotte Wright was found hanging from a beam in her bedroom by her sister, Melisa. Police were called to the scene at Iceberg Rose Cottage, Colbert's Field on the outskirts of Colbert Village, Essex at approximately 3:15pm. Charlotte, 29, had lived in the cottage from birth.

It is understood that her partner, Robert Mathews, was also living at the cottage. Mathews, we are informed by the police, is believed to have fled the scene and is now being considered as a person of interest. We understand that the police may be considering him as a potential witness to the hanging. They have issued a warrant for his arrest and are appealing to anyone who knows his whereabouts to come forward with that information.

Robert Mathews

The police have warned us that Mathews should be regarded as an extremely dangerous person and should not be approached under any circumstances.

Colbert's Field appears to have had a lot of bad luck over the years. In 1985 an elderly woman was beaten to death in Gloriana Rose Cottage. A year later, in 1986, a young woman visiting her grandparents at Sunrise Rose Cottage was brutally raped and murdered before being dumped in a river that runs at the side of the field. In 2000 a fire destroyed Alaska Rose Cottage. Although the occupants of that cottage were never found, it is believed that they were in the cottage when it was set alight. And now another potential murder has taken place in the same hamlet, in Iceberg Rose Cottage. My investigations have revealed that even before all these deaths the parents of an 8 year old boy living in Pilgrim Rose Cottage were murdered by their son!

Could all these deaths be related to the same person? Is there a serial murderer on the loose?

My contact in the police has informed me that it is too much of a coincidence that the deaths of all these unrelated people in the same hamlet occurred without there being some connection.

Police enquiries continue.

He knew this guy. He'd seen him before, not just at the field but elsewhere!

Looking at his watch he decided it was too late to meet up with Wally and Manning to give them the findings of his searches. It was also too early because he needed to call into the Observer's office to check on a couple of things.

Before leaving the office, he telephoned Wally and Manning and arranged a meeting at Wally's office for tomorrow afternoon. He agreed to call in at Colbert Village police station to pick up Sergeant Manning.

Chapter 36

Arriving back at the cafe, Mel greeted Bill warmly.

"Had a good time?" she asked.

"Not bad. Did some research. I'll show you later. First, though, I need to talk to you about something else. Is the kettle on?"

Mel nodded in the affirmative and they both went to the kitchen to make some tea. Returning to the table with a tray of mugs, the teapot and a few of Bill's favourite buns that Mel had baked, they both made themselves comfortable. A few sips of tea, a munch on a bun and Mel was, by now, bursting to hear what Bill wanted to tell her.

"Okay. Fire away. What's so important that you've taken me away from my kitchen?" she asked with one of her cheeky smiles.

Bill shuffled in his seat to buy some time while he thought of how to start.

"Are you any good at baking big cakes?"

"What do you think you're eating now?"

"That's not a big cake, that's a little bun. I'm talking about big cakes," exploding his hands to indicate big.

"Of course. Why who wants one. What type?"

"Type? Let's say a two tier… No, a three-tier cake, with lots of fruit and spices and icing."

"No problem. Expensive, but no problem. It's no more difficult than a wedding cake. Who's it for?"

Another pause, then, "Us…"

"Why would we want a wedding ca…" Mel sat back and eyed Bill through narrow eyes. "Is this a proposal?"

"About as close as you'll ever get to one," answered Bill.

"Well, the answer is no."

This hit Bill like a punch in the stomach. He looked down at his knees and thought how hard rejection feels.

"Oh. I'm sorry, Mel. I took it for granted that…"

Mel interrupted him.

"Quite right too, you did take me for granted. I was beginning to lose hope of you ever asking me, but the answer is no."

Another forlorn look from Bill. This time he started to collect his plate and cup to put back on the tray, then Mel grabbed his arm.

"Sit down, you big lump and wait 'til I've finished."

Bill sat and let out a long sigh.

Mel continued. "For a start, have you never heard of 'third time lucky'?"

Bill looked up with hope on his face.

"The answer is no, not until you get down on one knee and ask me properly."

For a moment Bill was confused. Then he realised that Mel was just winding him up. He got down on one knee.

"Melissa Wright. I love you. I have loved you from the first moment that I saw you serving customers in your rubber gloves and taking their money, and I thought to myself *'That woman will cook for me and wash my clothes and make my bed and clean up after me and I won't need to do anything in return.'* Will you marry me?"

"Of course, I will, but my services are expensive."

Bill's heart pumped hard as Mel drew him to her and gave him a long passionate kiss.

Bill asked, "Do you want a payment on account now?"

"You bet!"

They both retreated upstairs until the following morning.

The following morning, over breakfast, Bill told Mel about his resignation and his plan to become Mel's unpaid waiter and table wiper. She agreed to it with glee.

"But first," she said, "We need to make plans for our wedding."

They talked for a couple of hours, disturbed only once by a some hikers wanting some sustenance. They made initial wedding plans; who to invite, where to have the service, where to have the reception, what food to provide, that sort of thing, then Mel broke out of their idyllic discussion with a start.

"You were going to show me something last night," she prompted.

"Oh, yes. I forgot." He went to retrieve his brief case from the bedroom. Returning to his chair he took out the newspaper cuttings that he had printed off yesterday. Showing them to Mel, he asked, "Recognise anyone there?"

Mel studied the photos. After a few moments she said, "I'm pretty sure I've seen that man before," pointing to the one labelled with Robert Mathews name.

"When?"

"I've seen him on the high street. I was sixteen years old. I saw him coming out of the bank. It was about two or three days before I found Charlotte hanging in her bedroom. He looked at me with the smile of a perv' and stared at me as I walked home. I could feel his look on the back of my neck all the way to this place. He made my skin crawl. I don't think anyone in the village liked him. Mum told me all about him abusing Charlotte when I said that he had watched me come home, and she told me to stay well away from him."

"I'm pretty sure I've seen this guy recently," said Bill, "but I need to check something before I jump to any conclusions. I'm going to the Observer's office after breakfast and I'm back in London for a meeting with Wally and Sergeant Manning this afternoon. Fancy a day out?"

"Sorry. I've got a birthday party on for today, for one of the village's kids, and I've got a lot of prepping to do for that. Let me know what happens?"

"Will do."

Bill's trip to the Colbert Village Observer's office was productive. Joanna Smallbrook showed him to the archive room and left him to plough through the dusty files. Fortunately, the newspaper's archives were in a reasonably good condition, and he was able to extract three past articles.

The first one referred to Susan Brownlow's murder in1985. Although this article didn't tell Bill anything he didn't already know it at least substantiated Manning's version of events.

Colbert Village Observer - 13 May 1985

MURDER AT COLBERT'S FIELD

James Pensfield

An 85 year old woman has been found unconscious in the lounge of her cottage at Colbert's Field.

Mrs. Susan Brownlow was found by her daughter who visited her yesterday. She was taken to the A&E department of Colchester Hospital, but sadly died two hours later.

Police have opened up a murder enquiry because Mrs. Brownlow's injuries were indicative of a severe beating.

The local police sergeant, Michael Needham, said "The injuries to Mrs. Brownlow were particularly vicious and the offender is considered to be extremely dangerous and should not be approached. We are appealing to anyone with information to come forward. Statements will be taken in the strictest of confidence, and we can be contacted at any time, day or night, at Colbert Village police station."

The next article that he found was dated June 1986. This also confirmed Manning's version of what took place.

Colbert Village Observer - 23 June 1986

WOMAN MISSING FROM COLBERT'S FIELD

James Pensfield

A young woman was reported missing, this morning, from Colbert's Field. She has not been seen since 9:00pm last night.

Janine Potter, 18, was visiting her grandparents at Sunrise Rose Cottage when she disappeared. Her parents have been informed and they are now on their way to Colbert Village.

According to her grandparents, Janine went for an evening walk from their cottage shortly after tea, yesterday, but she didn't return after leaving through the front door. Her grandparents are extremely worried about her. Her grandfather told us, "She is a beautiful and caring girl who would not cause such a fuss. We pray for her safety . Her disappearance is totally out of character. She was in good spirits when she left us last night and we can't understand why she would disappear like this."

A search party, under the direction of Police Sergeant Michael Needham, is being formed. Anyone wishing to join this should assemble on Colbert Village green at 2:00pm today.

A television appeal will be made today at 6:00pm on all TV channels.

Police are appealing to anyone with information to come forward. Sergeant Needham can be contacted at any time, day or night, at Colbert Village police station."

It brought back memories of when Bill saw Ezra following Janine from her parent's cottage to the bridge.

With some sadness, Bill wished he could have prevented such a terrible event, but on reflection he reminded himself that when one is chasing ghosts of the past, there is not much one can do to change the course of history.

Bill's next find was a press release about the fire at Alaska Rose Cottage.

Colbert Village Observer - 5 July 2000

FIRE AT COLBERT'S FIELD

Shelley Dance

The Fire Brigade was called to Colbert's Field yesterday to attend to a fire at Alaska Rose Cottage.

The fire was reported by a neighbour who wishes to remain anonymous.

On arrival, the Fire Brigade were unable to extinguish the flames because the fire was so fierce and intense. Two firemen were injured trying to enter the building when burning debris fell onto them as they broke through the door. It was, therefore, deemed necessary to allow the fire to burn itself out.

A thorough search of the smoking remains was carried out by firemen in an attempt to locate the occupants but so far no remains have been found. A more detailed search of the debris, by the police forensic experts, will take place tomorrow.

As the occupants, a couple in their 40's, have not yet been located, the police have appealed for more information about them and the fire. It is, however, thought that the couple were consumed by the fire and it is doubtful that any remains will be uncovered from the pile of ashes.

Once again, Bill didn't read into this any more than he already knew, but he considered it good background to what he had to tell Wally and Manning later that afternoon.

Bill telephone Manning to see if he was ready to leave. After thanking Joanna for her hospitality, he made his way to the police station. Manning was standing outside waiting for him.

"I've just been to the Observer's office for some information," Bill declared. "You can go through it while we drive to London."

Not much was said until Manning had read every news cutting that Bill had put into a folder.

Looking across to Bill he said, "I've got much of this stuff on file, Bill, but it's always good to have more information. What else have you got?"

"I'll tell you in Wally's office."

The rest of the journey was spent in amiable chat between the two. Manning was taking a liking to Bill, and it seemed that the feeling was reciprocal.

Chapter 37

Bill, Wally and Manning made themselves comfortable in Wally's office. A tray of coffee and buns was placed on the conference table and light chat took place while the three men relaxed. They all had at least one file in front of them and they all eyed each other's file, waiting for someone to get the ball rolling.

Bill made the first move. "Good cakes, Wally. Must be rough at the top?"

"Don't know. Not got there yet."

"So, what have you got for us?"

Wally opened his file and spread its contents out in front of the gathering.

"First off, Bill, I've called in a favour, and we've managed to get Amy's phone unlocked. You owe me a drink for that 'cos my guy did it on the QT."

Bill re-filled Wally's cup. "There you go, Wally. Debt paid. What did you get from the phone?"

"Well, there are many intimate text messages between Amy and some guy. There are also quite a number of pictures of them together. I have to warn you, Bill, that the stuff we've pulled from the phone is not what you would expect from Amy. In the text messages she is clearly more than friendly with the guy."

"I know she was having an affair with someone at work," said Bill to put Wally's mind at ease.

"Okay. Well, the photos appear to be taken in the bedrooms of various hotels. Both parties are in a state of undress and they both don't hold back on any goings on.

Looks like the phone was propped up on a chair or something. There's a couple of videos, as well."

A brief moment of silence as they all inspected the photos…

Bill's inspection of the photos was brief. Very brief. He was slightly embarrassed about Amy's indiscretions, but he tried to make light of the findings. "She never did that to me."

Nobody laughed. The other two men appeared to be equally embarrassed, more so in Wally's case because he was Bill's best friend and Bill and Amy and himself had had many holidays, BBQ's, parties and dinner dates together. Wally was Bill's Best Man and vice versa, and both families were God Parents to each other's children. Wally had never seen Amy naked before these photos… And it showed.

Manning, on the other hand, scrutinised each photo carefully. It was much easier for him, being the outsider. He commented on how much the guy looked like one of Bill's press cuttings, more to break the embarrassing silence than anything else.

"What did you do with Amy's phone, Wally?" asked Manning.

"I've dropped the phone into Bill's office. Left it at reception."

"Anything else?"

Everybody shook themselves out of their thoughts and Wally answered, "Actually, I've got some good news. Our guys down at the lab have managed to enhance all that CCTV footage of hoody and they've got a better picture of him."

Wally produced another couple of photos from his file. They were slightly grainy, but the lab had made a good job of highlighting hoody's features.

Bill positioned the CCTV photos next to the telephone photos. All the men looked at each other and nodded in agreement.

"Yep." said Bill. "Definitely the same guy."

Manning asked, "Does anyone know this guy's name?"

Bill and Wally piped up at once, "Hugo," and then chuckled at each other.

Another question from Manning. "Hugo who?"

Again, Bill and Wally answered in unison, "Hugo MacEnrie."

Seeing Manning's puzzled look, Bill finished what Manning had asked. "Amy is… Was MacEnrie's co-worker. She was promoted to head of the science department over him, so he stayed head of nothing."

Manning continued to press Wally for more information.

"Is there any evidence that hoody started the fire?"

"Circumstantial only," answered Wally. "House-to-house enquiries have thrown up a witness that says he saw hoody walking towards your place, Bill, with what seemed to be an opaque plastic gallon container full of something. The witness couldn't say what it was filled with, but it was heavy enough to be some sort of liquid.

"Another witness saw him running to an Audi in the next street and getting into it, empty handed. He drove off at speed. The timeline between the two sightings is about fifteen to twenty minutes, enough time to murder Amy and torch the place. Both witnesses confirmed, between them, that it was the same hoody. Same clothes, same walk, same shock of blonde hair poking out of his hood, same guy. Crosschecked and confirmed."

All three men nodded at each other in agreement.

Bill opened up his file.

"I've not got a lot. Just press cutting from some research I've been doing."

He laid them out next to all the other photos.

"I know this guy," he added, tapping on the cutting discussing Charlotte's murder.

"Don't you think he bears more than a striking resemblance to Hugo?"

"He does," agreed Wally and Manning, "Although he calls himself Robert Mathews, there," Wally said.

Wally commented, "If Robert Mathews or hoody or Hugo or whatever he now calls himself has been rejected by Amy in some way, we may be able to use the photos, press cuttings and CCTV to substantiate a motive for killing her. Jealousy? Rejection?"

Again, all three paused to digest that last comment and ponder over Wally's questions.

It was Manning's turn to open his file. Placing several documents before them, he explained each one in turn.

"We have enough forensic evidence to show that the same guy was involved in several murders at Colbert's Field.

"Way back in 1975 Ezra Hugo Kendrick murdered his parents. This is borne out not just by Bill's news cuttings but by our own records kept at HQ. I never looked for this evidence because I didn't think about it until Bill started to make waves about what he had 'seen' at the field."

Bill looked down in embarrassment.

"Anyway," continued Manning, "this report, dated 1985," putting his finger on the first of the reports, "confirms that fingerprints taken at the scene of Susan Brownlow's murder match those taken when Ezra was detained in 1975. Whilst in custody his clothes were bagged up and put into the evidence locker for future reference. His fingerprints were all over the knife that he used to kill his mother and they matched the ones taken from the axe he used to kill his father. These were matched to those taken from his actual fingers. You know this already, Bill, but forensics reconstructed the bowl used to murder Mrs. Brownlow and they extracted Ezra's fingerprints from it," speaking to Wally. "So the youth you saw murdering Mrs. Brownlow, Bill, was eighteen year old Ezra. No doubt about it."

Bill and Wally looked at each other, then back to Manning to await his next gem of information.

Tapping the next report, Manning continued, "This is a forensic report dated 1986. Bill, do you remember me asking you if you recall what Janine Potter was wearing when you followed that youth down to the bridge?"

"Yes. Green, ankle length wellies, a floral-patterned dress and a gold top that shimmered in the late sunlight."

"Well," said Manning, "Forensics revisited the clothes recovered from the riverbank after I got them out of HQ's evidence locker, and guess what? Kendrick's fingerprints were lifted from her wellies. Forensics also managed to get some DNA from saliva they found on her top. Further still, DNA from two people was found on the outside of her dress. One sample matched Janine and the other sample matched DNA from clothes removed from Kendrick when he was detained in 1975. We believe he used her dress to wipe himself after raping her."

Wally piped up, "That's pretty damning stuff. You got anything else on this guy?"

"Indeed, I have. Recent comprehensive DNA testing has shown that Kendrick's DNA is present from the hair follicles found clutched in Charlotte's hand, when she was murdered. This, together with the DNA found from skin cells on the rope that was used to hang her, confirms Kendrick as the perpetrator.

"From all this, I reckon we can firmly assume that Ezra Hugo Kendrick is our serial killer. We have tied him to all the murders at Colbert's Field *and* to the fire that killed Amy."

Wally looked at his two guests. "From what we have all found out I think we have enough evidence to prove that Ezra Hugo Kendrick is in for a very long stretch in jail."

Both men nodded in agreement.

"Do we know his whereabouts?" asked Wally.

Manning replied, "From our records he's still on the run. Not been seen since Charlotte's murder in 2001."

Bill said, "He may still be on the run from you guys, but we now know that he's working at Amy's firm."

"Exactly," said Wally picking up the phone. Calling his secretary, he asked, "Can you telephone David March at Globe Publications and get Hugo MacEnrie's address and phone number?"

Replacing the handset, he turned to face his guests and asked, "More coffee?"

A few minutes later Wally's secretary tapped on the door and poked her head into the office. "Mr. March gave Mr. MacEnrie's home address as Pilgrim Cottage, Colbert's Field, Colbert Village, Essex. His phone is switched off, but Mr. March says Mr. MacEnrie left the office after getting a call from Miss Colbert."

When the secretary had left the room, Bill said, "That doesn't make sense. Those cottages were demolished in 2016."

They all sat and looked at each other for inspiration.

Bill broke the silence and asked, "Why the hell is she phoning him?"

Chapter 38

At the same time as Bill and Manning were meeting Wally, Elle parked her car and entered her office block.

As she swiped her pass card to get the entry turnstile to open the receptionist greeted her.

"Inspector Coombes has left a package for Bill. Can you take it upstairs for him, please?"

"Of course, thank you." replied Elle, taking the envelope from the receptionist.

In the lift, on the way up to her floor, she inspected the package. She felt what seemed to be a mobile phone inside the envelope. Putting the package on her desk while she took off her coat she thought about its contents. Knowing that Bill might not be back in the office for some time - maybe even a few days - and thinking the package might be important, she undid the string tie fastening the flap of the envelope and peered inside. It was, indeed, a mobile phone.

Taking the phone out of the envelope she put it on the desk in front of her.

Julie brought in a cup of coffee. "A new phone?" she asked.

"No. It looks like Mum's phone. Wally Coombes brought it in for Dad, but I'm not sure he's going to be back for a while."

Elle picked up the phone and turned it in her hand.

"What do you reckon," she asked, "do you think it's okay to turn it on and see what's inside?" a cheeky smile forming across her face.

Julie answered, "What harm can it be? Amy's not around to slap your wrist."

"That's true, but it's still private, isn't it?"

"Not any more…" Julie returned Elle's cheeky grin.

Elle said, "What if Wally Coombes wants Dad to keep the stuff on it a secret?"

"Then why did he put it in an envelope that's easily opened?" holding the envelope up by the flap string. "Tell you what, let me turn it on then you can claim that you didn't do it."

"Yeah… Okay!" handing the phone to Julie with a chuckle. She laid the phone on her desk.

Julie picked it up and pressed the 'on' button. The phone jumped into life then immediately went blank.

"You got a charger?" asked Julie.

Elle opened her desk draw and pulled out her phone charger. "I think this will fit," she said, handing the charger to Julie.

Phone plugged in; they both gave it a couple of minutes to get a small charge then Julie tried turning it on again. This time it opened up to show Bill's face on the front page.

Elle commented, "I'm surprised she didn't have it locked."

Julie replaced the phone on Elle's desk so that they both could see the screen.

Elle started by tapping on Amy's messages and began to scroll through them. There were lots from Amy to Bill, mainly passing the time of day letting Bill know that she was on the train to somewhere, or on the way home from somewhere. Suddenly, Elle came to a full stop when she saw a name that she recognised. The name was saved into its own folder and the folder contained many messages to and from this name. Elle hesitated before reading any of the messages.

"What's wrong?" asked Julie.

"I've got a bad feeling about this," she said. "I once caught Mum and a guy having illicit meetings."

"Do you think that's the guy?" asked Julie.

"I know it is." volunteered Elle. "That's Hugo MacEnrie. He works at Mum's place.

After reading the intimate text messages between Amy and Hugo the two women might have thought they were shocked. They should have thought again, because the photos and videos were more shocking than either of them could ever have imagined.

Julie could see tears welling up in Elle's eyes. "I'm so sorry," she said, placing a hand on Elle's arm.

Elle just looked at Julie, mouth slightly open, dumb struck for words to describe her reactions to what she had seen. Julie told her that she would go make another cup of coffee.

Elle sat down and turned the phone over and over in her hand. She slowly brought her thoughts back to the present and sat fuming at Amy. 'W*hy?*' she thought to herself. *'Wasn't Dad good enough for her? Didn't he give her everything he had to give? Wasn't his love for her enough? He doted on her! He loved her more than anyone. Why did she have to betray him like this?'*

Her anger rose inside her, twisting her stomach into knots and making her hands shake. Her mind was in a turmoil. *'Has Dad seen all this?'* she thought. *'It's going to destroy him.'* She picked up the desk phone and dialled Hugo's work number.

When the call was answered, she found it difficult to keep her voice from breaking.

"Can you put me through to Hugo MacEnrie, please?"

After a couple of seconds of silence, the telephonist returned to Elle.

"Who's calling?"

Elle gave her name, then another couple of seconds of silence. Hugo answered.

"Hi Elle. How can I help you?"

'Smug bastard,' thought Elle, *'What gives him the right to call me that?'*

"Hello Hugo. How are you?"

"I'm fine, thanks. How's yourself?" cheerfully.

'I bet he's fine.'

"I've come across some information about Mum, and I thought you might want to hear it."

"Oh, yeah. That would be great. What is it?"

As calmly as she could possibly sound, Elle asked, "Have you got time to come over to my office for a while. We're just around the corner. I've got a meeting coming up in a moment, but it shouldn't take long. We could have a chat and perhaps have a drink afterwards." she lied.

"Okay. I'll just wrap some stuff up here and then I'll be round. Twenty minutes, okay?"

"Yep. Great."

Elle returned the telephone handset and thought to herself, *'Let's see what the bastard has to say about this lot!'* putting Amy's phone to one side.

Bill, Wally and Manning were well into their meeting. Elle didn't know about the meeting, and she dialled Bill's phone to let him know who she was about to meet and what she was about to say to him. Her anger, by now, was reaching fever pitch.

Bill picked up his phone, saw who was trying to call him but turned the phone off without answering. *'I'll phone her later,'* he thought.

The landline phone on Elle's desk rang. It was Julie.

"Mr. MacEnrie is down in reception," she said.

"Send him up," replied Elle.

Elle sat behind her desk and waited patiently for Hugo to arrive. She took a deep breath and was determined not to lose her temper with him. She wanted to be as calm as possible, to watch the reaction on his face. There was a tap on the door and Julie poked her head into the office.

"Mr. MacEnrie," she announced and opened the door for Hugo to enter.

Hugo entered the room with a broad smile, thrust his hand out and said, "Hello, Elle. It's good to meet you."

'You won't feel so pleased with yourself after I've said what I'm going to say.'

Elle completely ignored his attempt at a handshake and remained seated. "Please, take a seat," she said nodding to her visitor's chair.

The rebuff took Hugo by surprise. He stammered a thank you, his smile fading, and he sat in the chair facing Elle.

He opened his mouth to speak, but Elle interrupted him. "Thanks for coming over," she said, surreptitiously placing a hand on Amy's phone.

"No problem," answered Hugo. "You said you had some info on the fire."

This response made Elle flinch. "No, I didn't say I had any information about the fire. I merely said, 'I've come across some information about Mum,'" picking up Amy's phone.

Again, Hugo was taken by surprise at Elle's indifference. "Oh, sorry. I assumed…"

Once more Elle interrupted his chain of speech. "You shouldn't assume so much," she said with a smile. "No, I thought you might want to see what is on Mum's phone."

Hugo was clearly agitated by now. He didn't like the way Elle had interrupted him, almost as if she was in charge, and he certainly didn't take too kindly to her off-hand approach to him. Who the hell did she think she was?

He tried to compose himself. "Erm... I... Are you sure it's okay?"

"Of course. She's not around to question it, is she?"

"Well, I suppose it's okay. Why do you want me to see it?"

Elle checked the charge rate and found a sufficient charge to unplug the phone. She opened up the messages and read a random couple to Hugo.

A *Am on my way to the hotel. Have you had your quota of oysters?*

Sure thing. Are you wearing you nickers? **H**

A *Nope. Are you?*

Nope. not enough room. **H**

You've got great legs! **H**

A *Have I?*

Yeah. And a great body! **H**

A *Anything else you like?*

Too true. You've got a great arse! **H**

A *Really?*

Yeah, and great tits - Best bit about you! **H**

A *Do you want to weigh them again?*

Yeah. When? Just say when. **H**

A *Usual place. 7 tomorrow night? I'll let Bill know I'm working late again.*

Oh boy! Room 252 here I come. **H**

Elle didn't need to quote any more messages to Hugo. She could see that he realised that the game was up. He sat back in his chair, all cocky and with a conceited air about him.

"So what? She was all over me."

Elle didn't respond. She just sat there, staring at him, anger in her eyes.

Hugo stared back for a second then shrugged his shoulder. "I didn't do anything she didn't want me to," he suggested.

This was Elle's cue to open up the phone's gallery and she pushed the phone over to him. He took up the phone and started to scroll through the images and videos.

With a smile he handed the phone back to Elle.

"You bastard!" she growled. "What's wrong? Can't get it up with anybody your own age?"

"Like I said, she was all over me." Hugo's bravado increased when he saw how much Elle had been upset with the images. "She couldn't get enough of me. In the photo-copy room, on the conference table, in her office, in my office, everywhere and anytime."

"You make me sick." She stood up and went round to Hugo's side of the desk. "You're nothing but a pathetic little runt who couldn't get a promotion. You're a leech." She spat in his face.

Wiping his brow with his coat sleeve he looked at Elle and calmly said "I wasn't the only one in the office, Elle. David March was enjoying himself with her as well as me.

Look at all the times he accompanied her on away trips, supposedly to meet clients."

Elle listened, stunned by what she was hearing.

Hugo continued, "And what about the client she so easily persuaded to give us his business. He certainly gave her his business, didn't he. So did that guy in the post room. Do you know, she sometimes went down to the wine bar at lunchtime to pick up a guy?"

"Stop it!" she screamed.

Hugo's anger had now also risen to an agitated level. His face took on a rambling look, his eyes wide and teeth bared in anger. Sweat began to roll down his face.

"It was all around the office. For the price of a meal, she was anybody's. She was everybody's. She was nothing but a scrubber. A dirty little tramp who prostituted herself to anyone who asked nicely. Brad Somerton even had a freebie whenever he liked."

This was like a punch in Elle's stomach.

"Liar!" snapped Elle.

Hugo's anger suddenly dropped down a notch. "I loved her, Elle. I begged her to leave Bill. Several times, but she kept refusing."

"She would never leave Dad for a pathetic clown like you."

Hugo ignored the degrading remark. His anger started to rise again.

He continued, "I knew about the client. He bragged to me one lunchtime, telling me what he did and how he did it. He told me she begged for more! He called her 'A slag!' I opened the door to March's office one morning and found her on the floor with that snotty little prat. She just stood up, confronted me and laughed. She said I was a nothing. A nobody. She told me my dick was too small to satisfy her.

When I found her with March, and the way she was being unfaithful to *me*, I was furious!"

By now Hugo was delirious. He looked as if he was hallucinating, spitting drool when he shouted. His eyes focused on some far-off planet and his collar began to darken with the stain of his sweat. Elle stepped away from him, worried that he might swing a punch at her.

As if he was in a misty trance, he looked at Elle with unseeing eyes and declared, "Can't you see, Elle? Can't you understand? When she said that I decided there and then that if I couldn't have her… Then nobody could have her."

Elle's eyes widened in horror and in a moment of realisation she quietly said, "You torched the house!"

Hugo smiled an insane smile, almost clown-like with large eyes and a smile that seemed to cover the whole of his face.

"She didn't feel anything, Elle. I made sure of that before I lit the match. I did check. She was definitely dead before I poured the sweet-smelling acetate over her. She wouldn't have felt the flames…" He looked pathetic, eyes wide open, tears streaming down his cheeks, yellow teeth showing under curled, smiling lips. It was as if he enjoyed the thought of Amy laying on the bed, burning to oblivion.

Elle snapped him out of his trance-like state. "You low-life bucket of slime. You need locking up forever."

Hugo calmly replied, "I did Bill a favour, Elle. I did all of you a favour. She won't be unfaithful to anyone ever again," with another far-off, smiley look in his face.

Elle snapped. She slapped Hugo across his face with all the might she could muster, then kicked him in his crotch. Watching him bent over in pain, groaning and holding his balls, she turned to see Julie standing in the doorway. Julie had witnessed almost everything that had happened.

"I've called the police," Julie said, "and the security guy is on his way up."

They both waited with folded arms until the security guy arrived on the scene. Hugo had picked himself up off the floor and was standing staring at the group.

"Hold him here until the police arrive," ordered Elle. The security chap nodded.

She then left her office to confront Brad. Julie returned to her desk to phone Bill.

Crashing in on a client meeting she stood staring at Brad, trying to think of something to shout at him. Brad turned to the conference table.

"Gentlemen, can we continue this meeting another time? It seems that Elle would like a word with me in private."

The clients stood, collected their papers and quietly left the conference room. When the door was finally closed Brad spoke up.

"What the hell are you playing at Elle? That was an important meeting."

"I've just heard about your *'friendship'* trips with Mum," dipping her fingers in the air. "Is it true?"

"Elle… I… Who's told you that?"

"Is it true?"

"I… Erm, I don't know how to answer that," hands turned palms up in front of him.

"So, it's true, you weasel. Some friend you are. No wonder you agreed to make me a Partner so easily. Were you hoping that I would be as accommodating as she was?"

"No, of course not. She came to me, Elle. I didn't need to make any move towards her. She was the one who started it. It meant nothing. It was just a bit of harmless fun."

"Harmless fun? I wonder if Dad would agree with that," she retorted.

Brad's secretary poked her head around the door frame. Brad waved her away.

He tried to appease Elle. "It really was nothing, Elle, but did you know she was going to leave Bill?"

"What? I don't believe you."

"It's true. Your dad was away from home so much. She needed someone to turn to. To comfort. A shoulder to cry on, and I can tell you, she cried often."

"Bastard! Rot in Hell!" was all that Elle could come up with. She turned and made her way back to her own office.

When she got there, she found Julie standing there, holding the telephone receiver in one hand and looking shocked. "What?" Elle asked.

Julie pointed to Elle's office.

Hugo had gone and the security guy was lying on the floor, unconscious. Elle picked up Amy's phone and threw it against the wall in utter frustration. It shattered into lots of pieces, spreading the parts around the room.

Julie came in to let her know that an ambulance and the police were on their way. "I tried to phone your dad, but his phone is switched off."

She retrieved her own phone from her clutch bag and dialled Bill's number.

Still turned off.

Taking her clutch bag and phone with her she told Julie, "I'm going to Wally's office. If Dad calls, can you tell him where I'm going?"

"Yeah, sure." responded Julie.

Julie stood quietly as she watched Elle depart from the office and enter the lift. When the lift doors closed, she tried Wally's number.

Chapter 39

Bill, Wally and Manning were sat pondering over Bill's comment about the absence of Pilgrim Rose Cottage.

"It does seem strange that Kendrick gave that as his address," said Manning.

"What's stranger is that Globe Publications didn't run a check on him or, indeed, his address. You would think that a big firm like that would want to cover their arses by finding out who wants to work for them," Wally queried.

Bill joined the conversation. "Maybe he put up a good enough case to employ him without checks. A case so strong that the boss didn't feel the need to delve into his past?"

"It happens," Wally replied. "God knows, we've had our fingers burnt on numerous occasions when one of ours has gone rogue. If we'd known about them from the start, we wouldn't have let them into the Force."

"So how do we find him?" asked Manning.

Wally thought for a moment and replied, "I'll put somebody in Globe's office to wait for his return. The people there can be interviewed at the same time. I'll also put out an all-points alert to keep eyes on the streets." He poked his head round the corner of his doorway and instructed his secretary accordingly. "Other than that, there's not much else I can do. We just have to hope that he doesn't go to ground again."

The telephone on his desk rang. It was his secretary.

"Sir, you've had several calls from someone called Julie, from Mr. Colbert's office. I've got her on hold now, and she's sounding a bit stressed out."

Wally asked the secretary to, "Put her through."

He turned to Bill. "I've got your secretary on the line, Bill. She's apparently panicking about something." He handed the phone to Bill.

"Hello, Julie. What's the problem?"

Bill could tell that Julie was crying immediately she answered.

"I'm sorry to disturb your meeting. I think you should come to the office straight away."

"Oh? Why's that?"

"Elle's just had a massive row with some guy called MacEnrie. I heard him admit to starting the fire at your place and…"

Bill interrupted. "Hang on, Julie. I want Wally to be in on this."

He motioned Wally to put the receiver on speaker and then returned to Julie.

"Okay, go ahead, Julie."

"Well, I was stood in the doorway to Elle's office when Elle was arguing with him, and I heard him say that he had started the fire at your place. He also confirmed that he had killed Amy before pouring acetate over her and setting it alight."

Bill looked at Wally. "That just about wraps it up for him, doesn't it?"

Wally nodded.

"What happened next, Julie?"

"I called the police and then told security to come up to the office. When the security guy arrived, Elle told him to watch MacEnrie until the police arrived…"

Wally interrupted, this time "Didn't he try to leave the office?"

"Well, Elle went to have a word with Brad, and I came out here to try to phone Inspector Coombes. I heard a crash and the next thing, MacEnrie dashed out of Elle's office and made for the stairway. I went into Elle's office and found the security guy on the floor, unconscious."

"Is he okay? Does he need any treatment?" asked Bill, concerned about the chap.

"I phoned for an ambulance, and they are taking him to hospital. I don't think he's recovered consciousness yet."

"What about Elle? Is she okay?" asked Bill.

"She left here to go to your office, Inspector, just after Mr. MacEnrie dashed out."

Bill took out his mobile phone. There were numerous missed calls from Elle.

"I'll phone her to tell her to get back to her office. We'll go over there."

Bill dialled Elle's phone but got no reply. Elle's phone just rang out until it pushed Bill's call to voicemail.

"She's not answering," said Bill.

Wally returned to his conversation with Julie.

"Okay, Julie. We'll leave here immediately and get over there as soon as we can. Let Brad know and try to contact Elle to let her know we're on our way."

With a sigh of relief Julie ended the call and sat down to wait for Bill to arrive.

On their way out of Wally's office, Wally instructed his secretary to let Elle know where they had gone if she turned up looking for him. The three men dashed down to the police car park, and they all piled into Wally's car. With blue lights flashing they flew across London, sirens blaring at the traffic to get out of their way.

Brad decided to go round to Elle's office to see if she had calmed down following their quarrel. He arrived just as the lift doors opened and two policemen exited the lift. Julie ushered them into Elle's office.

She began, "We've just had a guy called MacEnrie …"

"Yes, madam. We've been instructed to keep our eyes open for him. Where is he now?"

Julie repeated her story to the policemen who looked at each other and nodded. One of them backed out of the office and spoke into his radio.

The remaining officer held out Elle's clutch bag and said, "We found this lying on the floor of the car park. Does it belong to anyone here?"

With a gasp, Julie answered, "That's Elle's. She never goes anywhere without it. She left here with it in her hand when she went to go to Inspector Coombes office. She also took her phone with her."

Brad piped up, "Is her car still downstairs?"

"Don't know, sir. Shall we take a look?"

On the way to the lift Brad and the officer were joined by the officer's partner.

"I've radioed the details through to Coombes. He's on his way here."

Down in the car park, Brad took the officers to Elle's car, still in its parking bay. The driver's door was open. One of the officers held Brad back to stop him contaminating a potential crime scene while the other slowly made his way forward until he had an unrestricted view of the car's interior. Seeing nobody inside he backed off and unclipped his radio from his shoulder. Just as he was about to speak into it, Wally's car came into view.

Waiting until everyone in Wally's car joined them, the policeman gave Wally a quick appraisal of the situation then waited for instructions.

Wally instructed Bill to phone Elle again. Bill's call, once more, continued to ring but the ringing phone was heard by everyone in the car park. They all searched the area while the phone rang.

One of the police officers shouted, "Got it!"

Everyone turned to look in his direction.

The policeman pointed towards Elle's car. "It's there, under Miss Colbert's car," pointing, "Can you see it?"

Wally approached the car, got on his knees and reached under it, retrieving the phone with his finger and thumb. He took out a small plastic bag from his inside pocket and dropped the phone into it.

Returning to the throng he held the bag out to Bill and asked, "Recognise it?" He already knew the answer to that question, but he had to make sure.

With an alarmed look on his face, Bill replied, "That's Elle's phone."

Wally looked sternly at Bill. "Bill, I think we might have to accept that Elle may have been abducted by Kendrick."

Chapter 40

Everyone went back upstairs.

Bill and Wally split from the crowd and went to the security's den. Inside, they inspected the car park CCTV. This confirmed that Ezra had hidden behind a 4x4 until Elle had appeared from the lifts.

As she unlocked her car door, he snuck up behind her and grabbed her round the throat, hand over her mouth to stifle her screams. In the hand over Elle's mouth, he held what appeared to be a handkerchief. Elle put up a fight, but Ezra was holding her tightly. After a few seconds she slowly sank to the floor.

Looking round, furtively, Ezra then hooked his hands under her armpits and dragged her towards a row of cars. On the way Elle let go of her clutch purse but Ezra either ignored or forgot about the purse and dragged Elle out sight, to a car hidden behind a large 4x4 and unseen by the CCTV. Lifting the boot lid he bundled Elle into the cramped space, folding her legs so that he could close the boot. They didn't see the car move.

Wally nodded. "That confirms the abduction, Bill. Looks like he used chloroform to subdue her. All we have to do now is find out where he took her. Any ideas?"

"Nope, not one."

Wally asked for the CCTV frames to be fast-forwarded. The car drove forward from its parking bay, but it was hidden by other cars as it disappeared. As the image frames ran forward Wally put his hand on the security guy's shoulder and asked him to stop and rewind to film.

"Stop there!" ordered Wally. "See that?" he asked Bill.

The film had stopped at the exit barrier, showing the rear end of a car passing under the barrier arm.

"It's an Audi." said Bill.

"I recollect something about an Audi when we were reviewing CCTV back in May. Didn't a neighbour witness hoody getting into an Audi?"

"Yeah, I remember that", said Bill. "Just after another neighbour saw him carrying a plastic demijohn."

Wally asked the security guy for a copy of the CCTV, then turned to Bill. "I'll get DVLC to tell us who owns that Audi," pointing to the CCTV screen. "It'll confirm if it is Hoody or not."

The two men returned to the lift to go up to Elle's office. Manning was taking statements with the two police officers. Wally tapped him on the shoulder.

"Can you get onto DVLC and find out who this car belongs to? It's an early model Audi." handing a slip of paper to Manning. Manning disappeared into another office to make the call.

As Bill and Wally stood talking about the abduction Julie interrupted.

"Bill, I'm pretty sure we can track Elle. She wears one of those Fitbit watches."

As if a massive bell had just clanged Bill and Wally looked at each other with open mouths.

Bill asked Julie, "Can you access it from here?"

"Course I can. I do it often, when I need to know where she is so that I can let clients know how long she will be."

"Let's go," prompted Wally.

The three of them made their way to Julie's desk where Julie logged onto her PC and called up the appropriate software. A section of the UK was shown, with an arrow pointing to a road. The arrow was slowly moving in line with the road.

"Have you got an Atlas?" asked Wally.

"No need." Julie replied. Using the mouse curser, she exploded the image to get a better street identification.

The watch was tracked going along a small section of the A11 as it crossed over the A12.

Wally said, "Looks as if it's headed towards Essex."

Bill immediately recognised the location from the times he had driven to Colbert Village. He didn't immediately say anything in case he was wrong, and the tracking took them in another direction.

Manning returned. "The Audi definitely belongs to Ezra," he confirmed.

Wally got on his radio and put out a message for all cars to keep a look out for the Audi, giving its present known location. He ordered that the Audi should be stopped and searched, with the driver taken into custody.

As Bill and Wally watched the PC screen tracking the Audi, Wally asked, more to himself than anyone in earshot, "Where the hell is he going?"

The route that the Audi was taking, up the A118 towards Ilford, helped to make Bill's mind up about its destination.

"Are we sure that Elle is in the boot of that car?" he asked.

Wally looked up from the screen. "I'm as sure as we can be, Bill. We saw him bundle Elle into the back of a car in the car park, and we saw Ezra's car leaving the car park. Now, unless he's dumped her somewhere en route we have to believe that she is still in it. Problem is, we don't know where he's taking her."

The two men (and Julie) returned to the PC Screen. The closer the tracking got to Seven Kings; the more convinced Bill was that he knew its final destination.

Almost five minutes passed before Bill interrupted everyone's thoughts. Wally hadn't yet heard if any of the force had seen the Audi on its travels.

"Perhaps... Let's look at this from his perspective. He's been on the run since 2001. He never returned to the field. He couldn't, for fear of being recognised... He didn't know about the council's decision to demolish the cottages. As far as he's concerned, Pilgrim Rose Cottage still exists... He thinks that that cottage is still there."

The two men paused for thought before Wally concluded, "You're right!"

Chapter 41

Bill, Wally and Manning dashed back down to the car park and bundled into Wally's car. With Blue lights flashing and sirens blaring, Wally drove to Colbert Village breaking almost every rule in the Highway Code.

As soon as Bill managed to get a decent signal on his mobile phone, he dialled Mel's number and waited for a reply.

"Hello, Bill. How's things?"

"Mel, I need you to do something for me."

"Anything."

"We think Elle's been abducted and is being taken to the field. Will you keep a lookout for an old Audi passing the cafe?"

"Sure thing. I'll phone you if I see it."

"Mel, this is important. First, you must forget about what you're doing now and sit at the window to keep a lookout. Second, don't be seen and DO NOT, under any circumstances, approach the car. This guy is dangerous."

"Okay. What do you want me to do if I see it?"

"Phone me and sit tight. I'm on my way there now, with Wally. At this speed we should be with you in about forty minutes."

"Looking forward to that."

Bill terminated the call and sat back, worried about what Ezra had in mind for Elle. Wally put a call out for all patrol cars in the vicinity to converge on Colbert's field.

Fortunately, there were no customers to serve. Mel reversed the 'Open' sign, locked the door and sat at a table next to a window. She positioned herself just behind the window reveal so as not to be seen if the Audi came by.

She, too, was a little concerned that Bill thought Elle had been abducted and she worried if Elle was, in any way, injured. Elle and Mel had become good friends, especially since Bill had proposed, and Mel was beginning to look at Elle as her own. Mel didn't even make a cup of tea for herself. She just sat staring out of the window, hoping she could help both Bill and Elle, if help was needed.

There were six patrol cars on duty when Wally put out the call for backup. One was on the A406 dealing with an overturned truck that had spilled its contents over the dual carriageway, one was on the M25 dealing with an accident involving three cars and a caravan, one was on the M11 trying to get traffic moving after an accident, and three others throughout Essex; one in Chelmsford, one in Basildon and the third in Bishop's Stortford. Even with blue lights it would take a while for the cars to get anywhere near the field.

Manning radioed his young PC. "Get to Colbert's field as quickly as you can and keep a lookout for an early model Audi." He gave the Audi's registration number. "The driver is dangerous, so don't approach until backup arrives. If backup gets there first detain the Audi driver when it arrives and search the vehicle. There may be someone in the boot."

The PC confirmed his instructions.

Mel sat looking out of the window nervously. She saw Manning's young PC run by, heading towards the field. After about fifteen minutes the Audi chased by, going a lot faster than the permitted speed limit. She picked up the phone and dialled Bill's number.

"An old Audi has just shot by the window, but I managed to write down its number."

"What was it?" asked Bill. Mel repeated the number to him. "That's the one," responded Bill. "Sit tight until I arrive. I'm about fifteen to twenty minutes away."

Mel sat looking out of the window for a few seconds. Thoughts of Elle being beaten or worse, being killed, bounced around the inside of her head.

'I'm not going to sit here and do nothing,' she thought and decided to take some action of her own. Putting a coat on she left the cafe, after locking up, and made her way to the field. Walking briskly, she wondered what, if anything, she would do when she got there.

Manning's PC arrived breathlessly at the bridge. He walked through the open gates and slowly ascended the hill to the manor. He looked around for the Audi. Not there. The PC furtively walked up to the manor and looked through a couple of windows. Empty.

As he looked round for a suitable vantage point, the Audi suddenly appeared at the courtyard. Too late for the PC to hide, the PC stood in the middle of the courtyard with his hand held up in the usual gesture of 'Stop!'

The Audi didn't stop. In fact, it accelerated towards the young PC. Unable to get out of the way, the PC was thrown high into the air as the Audi ploughed into him. Landing heavily on the courtyard cobble stones he laid there, unmoving. The Audi slid to a stop in front of the manor.

Ezra got out of the car and walked back to the PC. He bent down momentarily to see if the PC was conscious then decided to finish the job. Taking a step backwards he kicked the PC's head as if he was taking a penalty at some competitor's goal. Ezra bent over the PC once more, straightened his back, nodded, then returned to the car.

He banged on the boot lid and heard Elle's protestations, interspersed with a few ripe expletives. Laughing, he looked around. With a look of surprise, it was obvious that his previous home was gone, and he stood for a few minutes, fists on his hips, thinking of a plan B that he hadn't thought of before coming here. Turning, to look at the manor, he decided that this would be a good place to implement plan B. He made his way to the manor doorway and entered, on the look-out for something to tie Elle up with.

He didn't see the shadow duck behind the window reveal in the bedroom.

Mel arrived at the bridge, looked round and made her way up the hill towards the manor. As she approached the courtyard, she saw the Audi standing next to the manor. Looking round, her attention was diverted to the PC laying lifelessly on the cobbles.

She was nervous now. Bill did say that the driver was dangerous, but she hadn't counted on seeing just how dangerous he was until she saw the PC. Her instinct to help the PC was stronger than finding a hiding place and waiting for Bill's arrival, and she silently made her way over to him. Kneeling down on one knee, with her back to the manor, she saw how the blood had oozed out of the PC's mouth and ears and was pooling on the cobblestones. His unseeing eyes stared, half open, at the sky. In the realisation that the PC was dead she gasped in disbelief, her heart pounded inside her chest as the adrenalin surged through her veins.

Mel then heard Elle shouting profanities from the boot and banging on the boot lid. She stood to go over to the Audi, but everything suddenly went black, and she dropped to the ground, unconscious.

Ezra had re-appeared from the manor holding a length of rope. He watched as Mel bent down to inspect the PC. Picking up a small rock he silently made his way towards her and knocked her unconscious as she stood to go to the Audi.

Now he had two women to deal with, a plan B he hadn't figured on, but so what? dealing with two women would be twice the fun.

Wally's car was held up on the bridge over the A406.

The overturned truck was proving to be more of a problem than first thought, because its load of chickens were flapping around, squawking all over the road and in people's gardens. The police were running around like chickens, themselves, chasing the chickens to put them back in the crates they had escaped from. Anyway, cars were backed up along the A406 and up the slip road as far as the bridge. Wally and his passengers sat waiting for a spare policeman to open up a route for them.

Ezra dragged Mel into the manor and tied her to a radiator. He looked round for another length of rope for Elle who had, by now, calmed down and was laying in the Audi's boot, waiting to be released.

Checking that Mel was secure, he returned to the Audi to get Elle. He banged on the boot lid, but Elle didn't make a sound. 'Oh well,' he thought, 'if she suffocated it'll save me the bother of strangling her,' remembering how he had smothered her mother before pouring acetate over her body and setting fire to it.

He shouted at the boot lid, "You're not going to do anything stupid, are you, like try and overpower me?"

"Get fucked!" returned Elle.

Smiling, Ezra said to himself, "I fully intend to…"

He unlocked the boot lid and carefully lifted it. Elle spat at him as she squinted against the bright sunlight.

"Feel any better for that?" questioned Ezra. "Get out!"

Elle swung her legs out and sat up. "You low-life bag of shit! Where are we? What are you going to do?"

"Patience, my dear. All will be revealed soon enough."

"I'm going to kill you, for what you did to my mum."

"I doubt it. Now get out!" he shouted, making Elle flinch.

She eased herself forward, staring ominously at Ezra. He gave her another warning.

"Do you want me to crack you on the head?" he snarled.

"No." volunteered Elle.

"Then do as I say and get out of my car. Try anything and I'll drop you so hard you'll never get up."

Elle's feet touched the ground, and she leaned forward to stand upright. As she straightened up Ezra grabbed her hair and dragged her towards the manor. She protested and pulled against his arm. Ezra stopped, lifted her head and punched her on the side of her head, just hard enough to stop Elle struggling against his grip and make her feel dizzy. He continued to drag Elle by her hair until they were inside the manor. He pushed her into the same room as he had tied Mel and then tied a woozy Elle to another radiator with a piece of rope he had prepared earlier.

The women sat in front of their radiators. Ezra had tied their hands back to the radiators, and the ropes were looped around their necks and dropped behind the radiator so that Ezra could tie the loose ends to the radiator pipes. Their feet and knees had been tied together. This, effectively, prevented the women from any movement.

Ezra went to Elle.

"You're almost as good looking as your mother."

This comment enraged Elle, but any attempt to release herself from the radiator merely tightened the rope around her neck.

Ezra laughed. "Your mother enjoyed a bit of bondage, Elle. I'm surprised you don't."

Elle gritted her teeth and tried to break free, but to no avail. She couldn't even lift a foot to kick him where it hurts. "Sick bastard!" she spat.

Ezra smiled an evil, leering smile. "Let's see if you are as attractive as your mother... was."

He ripped Elle's blouse open, exposing her bra. This was forcibly torn from her breasts. Ezra began to drool at the mouth. "Not bad." he grinned. "Not as small as Amy's, but nice and firm," dribbling saliva onto the front of his shirt.

He manhandled her breasts squeezing so hard that Elle cried out in pain.

"Ahh. Did I hurt you? I'm sorry," he declared insincerely. "Be patient, my dear. You'll soon know what real pain is..." he said, as he continued to fondle and lick Elle's breasts.

He stood back and looked Elle up and down. Melissa shouted at him, "Oi! Perv!"

This shook Ezra out of his manic trance, and he turned towards Mel.

"Oh, you've woken up," he chirped happily. "Wait there a moment. It'll soon be your turn," rubbing his hands as if he was warming them.

Turning back to face Elle he looked her up and down and said, "No, it's still not right."

He walked up to her and undid the press stud at the top of her jeans, releasing the zip he pulled both her jeans and her knickers down to her ankles.

"That's better," he mused as he took a step backward and leered at Elle's body.

Mel shouted, "You, sick shit!" trying to divert his attention from Elle who was now sobbing with a bowed head.

He looked at Elle, puffed out a deep sigh and went out to the car. He returned carrying a rag and a small bottle. He had, again, missed seeing the shadow duck behind the bedroom's window reveal. Approaching Elle, he unscrewed the lid of the bottle and poured some of its liquid onto the rag.

"I'm sorry, my dear, but I need to untie you and I'd rather you didn't struggle afterwards."

Putting the rag over Elle's mouth and nose he waited until the chloroform took effect and she sagged against her bonds. He untied her and laid her on the floor. After removing the remainder of her clothes and parting her legs he smiled at Mel as he loosened his belt and started to undress.

Wally's car pulled up outside the cafe. Bill jumped out and found the door to the cafe locked with the 'Closed' sign displayed.

Climbing back into the car he told the policemen that Mel wasn't in, and he sat back as Wally gunned the engine back into life. As the tyres screeched from a standing start away from the kerb, they heard the sound of police sirens announcing the arrival of their backup on the outskirts of Colbert Village.

Foot hard on the accelerator Wally steered his car along the lane to the field, directed by Bill.

When Ezra's attention had first turned to Elle, after dragging her into the manor, Mel had started to pick away at the knot securing the rope tying her hands together. In his haste to tie her up he hadn't tied Mel's bonds as securely as he should have.

While Ezra concentrated on preparing Elle for her rape, Mel worked away at the knot behind her back until she felt it loosen. As Ezra was removing Elle's jeans and parting her legs Mel found she was able to break loose from her bonds completely. As she silently untied her feet Ezra was drooling at Elle and taking his trousers off. Melissa heard the distant cry of Wally's siren as it approached the bridge.

Standing free of her rope, Mel shouted at Ezra as he was about to mount her.

"Get off her, you scumbag!" she shouted and threw some debris at Ezra's naked body.

A startled Ezra looked up and snarled, his yellow teeth bared behind curled lips, a wild look on his face, with slobber drooling from the corners of his mouth. A look that exposed how insane he was. A completely mad look on a completely different planet.

He stood to confront Mel.

Melissa started toward Ezra with the intention of putting up a fight. As long as she could pass the time until the police arrived, Elle would be safe. As they both got within arm's length of each other Ezra lifted his fist to throw a punch at Mel's face, then suddenly froze. This took Mel completely by surprise because she was expecting an onslaught from him, but he just stood there, eyes wider than wide, mouth open with his jaw almost resting on his chest.

Mel hadn't noticed the dark shadow slowly creeping up behind her... But Ezra had! As he backed off, Mel turned to see what he was so frightened of. She saw nothing. Turning round again to face Ezra, she saw him whimpering and shaking and pointing to something in front of him. With a puzzled look, Mel turned to Elle and started to cover her with her clothes.

As Elle began to regain consciousness Ezra backed into a corner of the room. He wailed, "You're dead! You're not real!" not believing what he saw. He was now a quivering jelly, cowering in the corner with his hands out in front, trying to fend off the dark shadow that engulfed him.

"Nooo…" he screamed. "Go away!" he screamed. "Nooo … Argh! …" He curled up into the foetal position and moaned and cried and slowly fell silent, his staring eyes focused on something only he could see.

At that moment Bill, Wally and Manning dashed into the room, hotly followed by several more uniformed policemen. Taking in the scene before them Bill was the first to move. He ran to Elle and cradled her head in his arms. Wally went over to Mel.

"What did you do to him?" he asked, looking at Ezra's quivering, whimpering body curled up in the corner.

"Absolutely nothing," replied Mel. "He just froze in front of me then backed off into the corner. He's been there, like that, since."

Bill looked up from tending to Elle. He caught site of Amy as she smiled at him and backed away into the shadows.

EPILOGUE

August 2025.

It's been a full three years since the murder of Amy Colbert at the hands of Ezra Hugo Kendrick. A lot has passed by since that fateful day.

You'll recall that Kendrick abducted Amy's daughter (Elle) and attempted to rape her at the manor on Colbert's Field. He was prevented from this terrible act by some unknown, unseen force. In fact, for no apparent reason Kendrick had withdrawn completely from himself and society in general. The police who arrived on the scene to see him whimpering away in a corner of a room in the abandoned manor could find no reason for Kendrick's insanity. The only witness, Melissa Wright (Mel to those who knew her), told the police that Kendrick just collapsed into the corner screaming, 'Leave me alone!', and 'Go away!', and 'You're not real!'

It is said that 'What goes around, comes around.'

Kendrick was taken from the scene in an ambulance and sectioned, for a second time, under the Mental Health Act. He is now detained in an asylum. In a twist of fate, it's the same asylum that he had inhabited after killing both his parents, way back in 1975. The same room even. He was eight years old, then, and he was kept locked up for a period of ten years. The committee that released him back in the day were, it seems, well and truly duped by his smooth talk into believing that he was safe enough to be released back into society. It turned out that they were wrong to believe that. He had callously murdered seven more people since his release.

Counting both his parents that's nine people, almost one person for every year that he was incarcerated as a child. A tenth person was saved by some unseen force that sent his mind to a distant, far off dark place. He had, it seemed, been pushed into a completely and permanently deranged state. Incurably mad.

This time round, the courts and the hospital authorities all deemed him unfit to ever be released. He now just lays in the foetal position, muttering unintelligible words to himself and shouting at anyone who enters his cell, 'She's there!' pointing to a blank wall. He is one hundred percent incontinent, so the staff have the unenviable task of cleaning him up every few hours. They also have to spoon feed him at mealtimes.

Sometimes his rantings are so constant and intense that the staff are unable to clean him up or feed him. At those times they have to put him in restraints, a straitjacket sometimes anchoring both wrists to the bed until he has settled down... As much as he ever settles down, anyway. They leave him like that for many hours, soiling himself, with him not caring about the mess or the smell. He probably doesn't even notice the mess or the smell.

Whenever the psychiatrists or hospital staff ask him who, or what, he can see all he answers is 'Amy!' wide eyed, scared out of his wits and pointing to some unseen figure standing next to his inquisitor.

From the evidence uncovered about the murders he was convicted, in his absence, and sentenced to life in detention with no prospect of release. Even if he was, at some time in the far-off future, released from the asylum, he would spend the rest of his life in prison.

But the diagnosis, for him, is bleak. For the time being, at least, he must spend his days lying on his plastic covered mattress, soiling himself, muttering words that only he can understand and staring wide eyed at a woman who constantly stays at his side, watching him, never speaking to him but just looking into his spaced-out eyes and smiling in torment. A woman who has never been seen by anyone else in the asylum.

What has happened to Elizabeth Colbert since she was abducted?

Well, she was one of the first to witness Kendrick's madness. She still reflects on what he did to her mum, and what he almost did to her, but she doesn't let it play on her mind too much. She is happy that justice has been (is being?) served.

She left her job at Colbert & Somerton... Now just called Somerton's, because she found out that a partner of the firm, a chap called Brad Somerton, had had an affair with her mum. At the time, Brad was considered to be a good friend of the family. Not anymore, though.

Elle is now a successful author. After she 'retired' from work she wrote a bestselling book about Kendrick's murders and how his downfall was brought about. A lot of the book focused on Bill's and Kendrick's association with the field and how the evidence that convicted Kendrick was assembled. The book sold worldwide, and the publishers are now pressing Elle for a another.

You'll recall that Bill inherited Colbert's field, along with a tidy sum of money, from one of his long-gone ancestors.

Having discussed what, he wanted to do with the field, with Elle, she decided to augment his inherited cash by placing an article about Bill's wishes on social media. A crowdfunding page generated a substantial sum for Bill's project, and he set about making the field a better place for people to visit.

He had the manor demolished and the resultant open space landscaped. In place of the manor, he commissioned a beautiful sculpture as a memorial to all the people that had lost their lives at the field, naming everyone. The memorial also depicted the five picture postcard cottages, each named after a different climbing rose.

In fact, the whole field was given a makeover. The remainder of the money pot had been used up with construction of a children's play area with a summer splash pool, and a family centre that the occupants of Colbert Village could relax in and enjoy.

Bill never forgot those five pretty cottages, with their rose bordered picture windows that hid the simplicity of the lives that lived in those cottages. Five cottages, all with secrets of their own. Five secrets, hidden behind those rose bordered windows. Secrets that had been long forgotten with the passage of time. Secrets that should never have been forgotten.

Bill has legally gifted the field to Colbert Village, with just three conditions;

- The first was that the village council would not now, or ever, build any houses on the field. If any houses popped up on the field it would immediately revert to Bill's ownership, or his nearest living relative if he had died.
- The second was that the council would maintain the field in its present condition, safe for anyone who wished to spend some time enjoying its facilities.
- The third was that the field should be renamed Rose Cottage Field, in honour of those who lost their lives on it.

Melissa Wright changed her name. She became, for better or for worse, Mrs. Melissa Colbert.

Bill and Mel's marriage ceremony was held in front of the memorial. They timed their marriage to coincide with the grand opening of the newly refurbished field. Hundreds of people attended the wedding and the grand opening. It seemed that the whole of Colbert Village had turned out, and many of the village's housewives contributed to the wedding feast, laid out on tables that stretched across the field and almost down to the Trout stream.

In the absence of any family, Mel was given away by Wally, now a Chief Superintendent and resplendent in his new uniform. Bill didn't have a Best Man. Instead, he had a Best Woman… Elle, who almost got Mel's wedding ring stuck on the finger she had used to keep it safe. Elle and Melissa are now inseparable friends.

Mel will shortly give birth to that baby brother that Elle had once mentioned to Bill.

Brad Somerton didn't receive an invitation to the wedding.

When Bill first arrived at the field for his wedding he stood around, like a spare peg, taking in the results of his labours. An old couple came up to him and casually mentioned, "I see you decided not to build any houses on it, then." Bill smiled, but just as he was about to speak, he felt a tap on his shoulders. It was George.

Bill turned to see who it was and held a finger in the air. "Hang on a minute George." He turned round to face the old couple, but they were gone…

Turning back to George he smiled.

George said, "Thanks for the contract to demolish that old manor."

"No problem, George. You deserved it." Bill replied.

George shook his hand, warmly and said, "I'm happy that you didn't build any houses on this field. It would have spoilt it."

For the first time since Bill met George, Bill saw George's perpetually grumpy face smile. A warm and sincere smile.

"I know." answered Bill.

After the wedding reception the village had its grand opening.

Everyone crowded round the stage in front of the memorial and listened as the village dignitaries thanked Bill for his generous gift and promised to comply with his wishes. There was lots of clapping and backslapping and when it was Bill's turn to make a speech, he approached the microphone and looked out, across the crowd.

Behind the throng, unseen by anyone in the crowd, Bill saw a small group of people standing watching the ceremony. The sight of this small group almost made Bill forget his lines, but he said what he had come to say and stood there as the people of Colbert Village applauded him.

Everyone in the small group waved to him. Susan Brownlow, Janine Potter, the couple from Alaska Rose Cottage, Peter the young PC, and the old couple that Bill so often met taking a walk in the high street - Sergeant Manning's parents. Standing tall in the centre of the group were Charlotte and Amy. They all waved a goodbye to Bill as they faded away to nothing, leaving a blank space where they had been standing. Bill waved back. The villages all thought he was waving to them.

But Bill knew better…

Table of Contents

europe books